ALIEN PROTECTOR'S RESCUED BRIDE

JUNO WELLS

CONTENTS

FOREWORD

Alien Protector's Rescued Bride is a stand-alone but is part of the Draconian Warrior's Series.

You'll enjoy it more if you start at the beginning!

Alien Warrior's Captive Bride

1 CAGED

DAISY

I wake up gasping for breath. I'm being dragged along by a cold clammy hand wrapped around my upper arm. Somehow I'm walking but my legs keep buckling beneath me, causing me to fall to my knees. My handler is an angry aquatic and he's got no time or interest in giving me a minute to get myself oriented.

My alien abductors have apparently taken me out of hibernation again. I don't know why they take me in and out the way they do. It's damned annoying, but I force myself to acquiesce to their demands. Forcing my naked body to move at his pace takes one hundred percent of my concentration and energy.

The aliens drag me to another room and toss me face-first into a small cell. Actually, it's more like a cage, with metal bars around the sides and top. I collapse onto the ground, a shaking, wet mess. I'm always cold. Maybe it's because they never see fit to clothe us. Or perhaps it's because outer space is freezing and they aren't wild about wasting precious resources on beings they consider cargo. I hate everything about being on this ship with these cold ruthless aliens.

My life got turned upside down the night they came for me. One moment I was a communications specialist for the Northern United Provinces on Earth. It was a really good job. I got to wear a cool corporate uniform and everything. Heck, my uniform was even sharper than the ones worn by the United Earth Military unit I'd been assigned to work with. Earth now had one gigantic military and every province was required to contribute soldiers, supplies, and adjunct personnel like me to ensure mission readiness at all times. Too bad we didn't get any real military training or I might have been able to fight off my abductors. I wasn't, so now I'm just another abductee.

They've got dozens of us—mostly human—but all female. I already know selling human slaves is brisk business. When Earth made first contact about eight years ago, humans seemed to be broken into two camps. Most were charmed with the aliens that visited our world and fascinated by the tech they shared with us. A smaller percentage of Earth's citizens were terrified of our new visitors, especially after women started turning up missing. Earth Military Command sent out warning bulletins for every citizen to be careful of unknown alien species. They restricted landing privileges and that seemed to solve the problem, or so we thought. After being abducted myself, I now think the military just lied to keep everyone from panicking.

It was good advice, because I sure don't know anything about the aquatics who stole me away in the night. They're short and stout with clammy hands and fins that poke out of their heads on either side. They have oversized black eyes and no visible body hair. The subtle scale pattern on their skin would give away their aquatic heritage even if it weren't for the fins.

A female voice calls out to me. "Hey, are you okay? You look like shit."

Rolling over to face the other woman, I see she's human. My best guess is she's from the Eastern Provinces, maybe Asian from the jet-black hair and almond-shaped eyes. Her thin body is on the floor. Squinting at her, I can tell that she'd be considered beautiful if not for the greasy hair and grime covering her body. Of course she's buck naked and sitting with one knee bent and her arm resting on it.

From my vantage point, I can see everything God gave her. Pushing up from the floor, I croak out dryly, "Good grief, put that thing away."

She laughs and pulls her legs closed. "Sorry, I've been without clothes for so long that sometimes I forget how naked I am."

Struggling up to a sitting position, I tuck my legs to one side in an attempt to retain a modicum of dignity. "I didn't mean to be rude."

"I haven't been in the tank in years." Gesturing around the room with one hand, she adds, "I gotta say, it's damn hard to stay modest around this place."

Running my hands though my wet hair, I continue, shivering. "My name's Daisy Callahan. I don't think I've seen you before."

"I'm normally in their alien version of solitary confinement. My name is Meiko Hara. I love the southern accent by the way. It's cute on you."

Covering my breasts with my arms, I try to force myself to stop shaking. "You don't have a trace of an accent, Southern or otherwise."

"My parents are from Maine." A dark expression jumps

onto her and then is gone in an instant. "Well, we were from Maine until our life turned upside down. I'd just started my degree at UMO when my father didn't come back from a business trip. After that, it was just me, my twin sister, and my mother. She probably thinks we abandoned her when the going got tough, but my sister and I would never do something like that."

I'm thoroughly confused by that idea. What are the chances the aliens abducted them both? Logic sweeps down my foggy brain, quickly realizing that if they were both together, the aliens could very well have taken two as easily as one. "You have a sister here?"

"I *had* a sister here. One day I woke up and she was gone. After that, let's just say I gave those stupid aquatic bastards a run for their money."

"If you fought with them, you lost. I ought to know because the same thing happened to me."

A dark look crosses her face. "Sometimes, it's not about winning so much as making the entire experience painful for them." After a brief pause, she continues. "I never found out what they did with my sister, but I've made them bleed that cold black shit they call blood more than once."

"I never managed to inflict any real damage on them. They just beat the everlovin' crap outta me until I lose all interest in resisting."

Her head tilts to one side and her chin comes up slightly. The stubborn expression on her face speaks volumes about how she'd never wimp out like me. "Don't worry about it. I'm giving the fishy bastards enough hell for both of us. I don't remember how they got me, but I've made keeping me a pain in the ass for them." Relaxing back against the wall fully, she asks, "What's your story? Did they get any of your family when they took you?"

"God no, I lost my parents and brother in a flood off the Carolina coast two years after the oceans turned sour." My voice drops and my throat almost closes up at the recollection of that day. "We were laughing and joking one minute and they were gone the next. It seemed surreal at the time."

"How were you abducted?"

With my bottom lip quivering, I launch into the relatively short and absurd story of being snatched while driving from one of the huge city-sized bio-domes to a military compound out in the Arizona desert. "Anyway, there were no alien ships dropping down out of the sky or teleportation beams. A bunch of aliens surrounded me on a long lonely stretch of highway. They seemed to come out of nowhere. Even with the limited amount of training I had in hand-to-hand combat in preparation for working as a liaison with the military, I never had a chance. There were too many and they were twice my size."

Leaning forward slightly, her mangy hair slides over one shoulder. "Let me guess... You woke up pounding on one of those damned hibernation units?"

"I sure did, not that they gave two hoots in hell. They just went on about their business without a care in the world." My body is not cooperating. The trembling is not easing up. Instead, my hands are jerking involuntarily and I feel like I'm about to have a seizure.

Suddenly, the door slams open and Shark Eyes strolls in, dragging a hover board behind him. Now, I know his name isn't really Shark Eyes. That's what I nicknamed him in my own head because of the black beady eyes. He's our handler, for lack of a better word to use. It's always the same. Whichever one of them takes me from is the only one I have contact with until I go back into one of the hibernation units.

Today he appears to have space blankets. The moment he tosses one through the bars, I tug it open with shaky hands and pull it tight around my body. It reminds me of those silver emergency blankets rescue workers wrapped around survivors on Earth. Only this one is stretchy and has a slight fishy odor; then again everything on this ship does. Settling down, I watch him rummage through the things on his little hover board.

Yay! He's also got the watery soup that qualifies as both food and water. It's normally cold, fishy-tasting, and thoroughly revolting. He rolls a clear canister to me and then to Meiko before squealing a laugh and heading back toward the door.

Reaching out to grasp the canister, Meiko gasps. "It's hot. Do you have any idea when I last had hot food? It only happens occasionally and tonight's our lucky night."

It takes me a moment of fumbling to get my hand around the canister. "What makes you think that it's night?"

For all we know it could be daytime in the aliens' sleep cycle. Wrapping one blanket-clad arm around the canister, I press the lid to get it to release. Whatever they're feeding us sure smells better hot. Bringing it to my mouth, I tip a small bit in. "Oh my God, this is amazing." Glancing at my dining partner, I add a disclaimer. "I mean it's amazing compared to what they normally feed us when we're out of hibernation. It' not as good as grits or chicken-fried steak, but it's better than the cold stuff."

Meiko takes a long drink from the canister before wiping her mouth on the back of her hand. "What in the fresh hell is chicken-fried steak?"

Since I was taught not to gulp and I feel like I might hurl if I drink too fast, I continue to sip. "It's steak that's batter-dipped and fried like chicken. It's usually served with white gravy on top, sprinkled lightly with fresh black pepper."

Her face pulls into an expression of utter disgust. "I think I'll stick with warm alien soup."

"You don't think they're cannibals, do you?"

The other woman's face contorts into an expression of bewilderment, so I explain quickly. "We've been abducted by a race of aliens with strong amphibian traits. Don't you think it's strange that they're feeding us this watery soup with bits that taste like fish?"

"What the hell are you saying?"

I shrug noncommittally. "I don't know. We've been on this ship for God only knows how long. What with the taking us in out of hibernation, there's no telling the passage of time. I'm guessing it's been a long time or they wouldn't need to put us in hibernation. Maybe our soup is made up of Finny, who passed after sustaining an injury while trying to make a complicated engine repair."

Her eyes narrow on me in a disapproving manner. "You're being absurd."

I almost can't keep the smile off my face. Honestly, my lips haven't warmed up enough to even think about smiling. "Maybe they're not cannibals and it's just us they feed their fallen crewmen to."

Shooting me an annoyed look, she takes a nice long drink of her soup and opens her mouth to show me she's eating the fishy bits. "If they are feeding us people then all the better. I'll dine on the stupid unfortunate bastards all day long with a smile on my face."

"You really hate them, don't you?"

"Hell yes. Tell me you don't."

I lean forward, holding my cylinder of soup out through the bars. "I'm right there with you, girl."

The corners of her mouth tilt up and she reaches her cylinder out to clank roughly against mine. "To hell with the fishy bastards, I say."

I manage a wane smile as I drag the conversation back to food that's actually palatable. "So, no chicken-fried steak for you. Don't you miss any food from Earth?"

"I do miss seafood, good quality lobster especially. I haven't had any for years, since the oceans turned bad." Her wistful expression has me reminiscing about everything I miss about Earth. Though she's a hollowed-out dystopian husk of her former self, Earth is still home in my mind. I know some women signed up for the Brides registry, took alien husbands, and are living the good life on some pristine alien planet. Unfortunately, my life doesn't appear to be on any kind of trajectory that might involve home and hearth.

Worry gets the better of me and I ask Meiko, "What do you think they're gonna do with us?"

Looking me in the eye, she responds succinctly. "We're going to be sold for sex or food. I honestly don't see any other outcome."

Her straight-shooting answer to my question is a real come-to-Jesus moment for me. Then I wonder if she's talking about them using us for food because of what I said about our captors potentially being cannibals. I clearly should not have planted that idea in her head. I have more scenarios running around in mine than just the two.

Meiko's voice turns harsh, leading me to believe she doesn't suffer fools gladly. "Don't act so freaking surprised, girl. I've been trying not to interpret that slow Southern drawl of yours as evidence of a low IQ, but no matter how slow you are, you gotta know sex and food are about the only reasons aliens would want people like us." Frowning, she goes back to eating her meager dinner.

Normally, I'd be ten kinds of angry to hear someone making disparaging comments about my heritage. Yet, it's impossible for me to have hard feelings toward a fellow human being sitting in a cage and eagerly chowing down on what I suspect is alien garbage. I don't have it in me to fight with her right now about her stereotypical thinking. Bracing my hand against my stomach, I realize something horrifying. For the very first time in my life, I have no fire in my gut. It feels like my spirit has been broken and I don't know how to put it back together again.

Since I don't have any fight left in me, I take a more rational approach. "I think it's logical to assume we'll be sold for food or sex, but I can think of other options. Rich people enjoy displaying expensive ornaments. Perhaps some wealthy alien might buy us to keep as pets and show off at dinner parties."

Meiko's eyes find mine and she's surprised. "I doubt anyone would think to do something so absurd."

"When I was in the United Military, we were briefed about a drug lord who kept an enemy for years, slowing starving him to death. He had the corpse mummified and used it to decorate his villa. If some alien makes an ornament out of me, I hope they want a nice attractive fleshy one."

Meiko busts out laughing. "Girl, you caught me off guard with that one." Draining the last of her warm soup, she shakes her head. "I guess we might be bought for ornaments."

"We might end up being slaves to some alien who doesn't like to do chores."

Meiko snorts another laugh. "Maybe, but I don't think they'd consider humans resilient enough to perform hard labor."

"You're right about that. Hell, every alien I've ever set eyes on is bigger and stronger than a human."

Meiko chimes in, "They definitely see us as weak. I can tell because they've made the mistake of turning their back on me more than once."

My chest deflates and my shoulders droop. "They ain't wrong about that either. Compared to them, we are kind of pathetic."

Cocking her head slightly in the gesture I'm coming to associate with defiance, my companion taps the side of her head. "We might not be able to hold our own in a physical battle, but we're smarter and more creative than the freaks who took us."

A short silence spins out between the two of us as we look each other in the eyes. I really like this quirky stranger, and if the admiration and growing respect in her dark eyes is any indication, I'm growing on her as well.

I break the silence by verbalizing my secret wish. "You'll get no pushback from me on us being smart and crafty. Still, it would sure be nice if we got sold to regular aliens looking for a bride."

Meiko's expression lights up. "It sure as hell beats every other alternative we've talked about."

2 SILENT PROTECTOR

DARNOK

Jolting awake from another dark dream, I can't get my head straight. Fuzzy memories of horrific injustices distill into fully formed memories. My mind is assaulted with images of our former queen reaping her hatchlings. Though I've never been chosen for mating and am no breeder, memories of Rovanda squashing the little ones in their shells haunts my every walking step. The ghastly images come unbidden when I am awake and asleep. Nothing I do is effective in making them go away.

I am shamed by own lack of self-control. Who among the warriors would believe the great Darnok would be affected by such things? I've faced down countless enemies in combat, fought alone against hordes, and have never known defeat on the battlefield. Yet, mastery of my own mind completely eludes me.

It matters not, for now we have a pale human queen. She's fierce in defense of the young aboard this vessel. Queen Cassandra ripped us from the clutches of our former queen and we now know the luxury of being equally valued by our leader. Humans see no differences between breeders and warriors, as evidenced by the fact that she chose a simple warrior as her *takadon*. Her mate showed his worth and was rewarded by being chosen as her one and only breeding partner. Though Queen Cassandra would not recognize me by sight among the thousands of warriors under her command, she has earned my respect.

I roll over, pinching my wing beneath my heavy form. Tugging it free, I toss my legs over the side of the sleeping platform. I bump over onto one buttock to free my long thick tail and drop back down. My muscles ache, as do the multitude of scars covering my body. Each scar comes with a memory. Some make me cringe while others inspire fierce pride. No one but me knows which are from battle and which are from abuse by our former queen. Her claws were made to rend flesh and mine was a prime target. I am the largest of my kind, a behemoth among warriors. Our former queen used to love digging her claws into me just to prove she could.

The door to my tiny private sleeping room slides open and Roan strolls in. His wings are relaxed and his horns are drooping back slightly. He continues dressing like a breeder, though our new queen acknowledges no hierarchy among males.

The long flowing pants seem more like a gown than the garb of a male. However, his finely chiseled chest announces his masculinity fairly effectively. The fanciful image inked down the right side of his body represent elements of his lineage. I am poorly designed by comparison, all bulky muscle, oversized wings, and crude markings.

Frowning at me, he stops short in the doorway. "Darnok, do you yet sleep? How can you slumber idly when there are so many tiny queens to see?"

Standing, I stretch, wearing only the scales the gods

have given me. "Unlike you, I have no wish to while away endless microns staring at the tiny creatures. My size draws notice and with it, expressions of fear and revulsion from all the new human queens."

"Get dressed. If your size causes fear, the sight of your rod will surely stir a panic among the lovely humans."

Looking down at my weighty morning erection, I can see his point. Chirping out a rare laugh, I grab my uniform and put it on quickly.

Roan gestures for me to hurry up as he exclaims excitedly, "Thanks be to our new queen for rescuing so many of her kind. I never thought to see so many females all in one place. They are all sizes and shapes. This morning, I even saw one with beautiful skin as dark as the night sky. Her hair stood out around her head like a fine soft mist. I could not take my eyes off her until she passed. There are queens everywhere I go and none wish us ill will."

The sound of amazement in his voice mirrors my own. The human queens are tame, to be sure. "It is good to see them safe and wandering around our ship, enjoying the first taste of freedom they've had in a long time."

"Then why are you so reluctant to mingle with them?"

Swallowing thickly, I speak words to Roan that I would share with no other. "A small part of my soul shrivels up and dies every time I see their reaction to me. The looks of horror and revulsion followed quickly by pity is difficult to see on their pretty faces." Stepping into my boots, I move forward to stand face-to-face with my friend of many solars. "I have no wish to affect them so. Though I wish it were not so, I am a monster in their eyes."

Reaching out, he grasps my shoulder and squeezes slightly. It is a show of solidarity and understanding, not pity. Roan is perhaps the only one among the warriors who truly understands me and for that I am grateful. "You have a kind and gentle soul, Darnok, and always think of others first. It is the reason Rovanda visited so much misery upon you. She knew we were close and your tender soul was wounded by watching her reap my young."

Covering his hand with mine, I fight to keep control of my emotions. "At least you yet have young, unlike Pern who was left with nothing."

"Even now he isolates in his quarters, preferring the solitude of his tiny room to the company of queens."

"You should burst through his door and cheer his soul."

His hand drops from my shoulder and one side of his mouth tilts up in a lopsided grin. "Do not think to turn my attention to other males. I have decided that I will not rest until you are chosen by a queen."

I cannot keep the laughter from spilling forth. "That is too absurd an idea to even draw images of it in my mind, Roan. You are twice the size of a human queen and I am larger than you. Such a thing would not possible, much less advisable."

"We now have four ships in the armada."

"Queen Rovanda would explode to see Queen Cassandra sitting in her chair on the bridge."

Roan grins. "As would Queen Heinka to see Queen Tela at the helm of her former ship."

I warm to the idea that even the younger queens have ships. "Young Bejkatonda leads the training ship with the support of her father, and Queen Aiko controls the aquatic vessel we seized with young Queen Nanabella at her side."

"It pleases me to know that our queen reserved ships for the young Draconian queens. She could have chosen human queens to rule."

"I must give the human queens credit where it is

deserved. They are nothing if not fair-minded regarding our two young queens. Joining together in an armada goes a long way in ensuring their safety in this new sector of space."

"After conducting a fair amount of research on this sector, I found but few predator species, and only a handful have access to space. It's reasonable to believe our safety will be easily protected."

"That is what everyone says, but I think where there are queens congregated together there will be males wishing to steal them away."

"We will know soon enough if such things come to pass. Come along, my friend. Let us find work so the goddess might smile on us this day."

Roan is back to being all smiles and I am happy for him. "I will work, but I want you to assist me in devising a way to serve the queen with the hair like soft mist."

I can hear the eager excitement in his voice and it's good to see him trusting in the good will of a queen once more. At one time Roan only wished to avoid the notice of his queen. Human queens are what the goddess had in mind when she created females. I can only think she failed in creating Draconian queens in their image.

Since breeders now work like normal warriors, we seek out manual labor in the loading bay. It is the place where special projects are located. There are more warriors than assignments these days. Upon arrival we discover that Queen Cassandra has commanded that there be trade for supplies for our voyage to Earth. She demands foodstuffs, medical devices, and fuel be procured. Takadon Mathadar is standing in the center of large group of warriors, all wishing to be chosen for this assignment.

His eyes land on me and his chin jerks up. "Darnok, Odem, and Ralen, step forward."

Shooting Roan an apologetic look, I trot over to speak with our queen's takadon. "I have had three shuttles prepped and have arranged for some of our mineral stock to be traded for Ragelian credits. Darnok, I wish you to drop off the minerals at the Ragelian trade center, load their credits into our account, and draw out only what you need to secure the medical equipment and supplies we desire. Before you ask, she is not seeking Tarken. The beings of this sector of space have no knowledge of such debilitating drugs and our queen would not partake of such even if we had a supply on hand."

Bowing my head slightly, I murmur, "This I know, Takadon Mathadar. Our new queen is nothing like the Draconian queens."

His dark expression clears. "She wishes to save the lives of as many of her kind as possible when we arrive at her home world. You will trade with an eye to saving the lives of queens."

"Our queen's will be done, Takadon."

I know our new queen would never take illicit drugs. Our former queen was unique in that regard and it cost her the command of her ship in the end. I still remember watching their escape pods shooting through space before being sucked into the upper atmosphere of the planet they were to be marooned upon. It was the first taste of real justice I had known in my lifetime, and I relish the memory even today.

Turning his attention to the remaining warriors, he continues, "Odem, how is your sister aboard the *Delacroy*?"

"She is currently sequestered with her own takadon,

Trace. All is well aboard our ship. Thank you for asking, Takadon Mathadar."

"I am pleased the young queen is well. We need food-stuffs fit for the belly of a queen, and as you well know we have many queenly bellies to fill."

Odem's face lights up. "I have never seen so many queens, especially ones who issue no challenge to each other. Even my sister queen, Tela, has no wish for conflict with the other females."

"It is strange to see them walking together and laughing. It almost seems as though they enjoy each other's company." The expression on Ralen's face matches the wonder in his voice.

Mathadar's mouth twitches as though a smile is trying to get out, but he holds it back. "I think of human queens as behaving more like warriors in that regard."

To my mind that means they have friendships and bond with one another. It is a strange concept, but I have seen it with my own eyes. Therefore, I have no doubt what he says is true.

Ralen nods. "What would you have me do, Takadon Mathadar?"

Mathadar responds succinctly, "Your job is fairly straightforward. Obtain the medical supplies we need to make this journey and enough in reserve to make sure we are not short if we incur causalities due to unforeseen circumstances."

He has tasked me with an important job, one that I cannot fail because lives may be lost if we do not acquire the items needed. "I will see it done."

Mathadar assigns twenty warriors per shuttle and we begin the lift off procedural check. I can hear Roan arguing with our commander over not being assigned to go down to the planet. From what I can tell, Mathadar is concerned that he's not battle ready. Roan is a breeder. He's not been keeping up with his training, since he's spent the last twenty cycles worrying about pleasing our former queen. Pulling out my com, I peck out a message for our commander.

Roan has no queen to attend to. He needs purpose to recover from his ordeal as Rovanda's breeder. Let him come. If it pleases you, I will take him under my wing.

I watch as he pulls out his comm and reads my message. He knows as well as I that we are visiting a friendly planet in human space. It is highly unlikely that a battle will ensue. This is the safest mission in which Roan could ever hope to partake, so I am not all that surprised when Mathadar steps forward into Roan's personal space.

Though he's smaller than my best friend, the commander radiates power. They have words that I cannot hear because Mathadar has lowered his voice. Roan's expression changes from angry to excited. He speeds toward my shuttle and my spirit lifts. Breeders were never allowed to leave the ship under our former queen, so this is a new opportunity for Roan to see an alien world.

Climbing on board, the other warriors shuffle over, making room for his larger form. I am glad to have him along. With another bulky warrior I don't feel like I'm playing toy warriors with the assembled crew. Our communications units sound off and we pull them out to scroll through the list of medical supplies we are to seek out. Roan is enthusiastically scrolling faster and paying way more attention than any of the other warriors. Yes, I believe this is going to be one of our easier missions.

All our heads come up as we break cloud cover and descend into the lower atmosphere. We all lean forward a bit as an image of the landscape below comes into focus. All planets are beautiful in their own way, all except this one. It is nothing but sand and utilitarian buildings made from metal. There is no vegetation or water in sight.

The only one among us who manages to remain enthusiastic is my good friend Roan. The other warriors are frowning or groaning their disapproval. Since he's never been on a planet before, Roan must think this one is just amazing. Maybe it is and we're just difficult to please, I think to myself. It does not matter so much to me if the planet is pleasing, for I am happy to do the will of my new human queen.

3 LAST STAND

DAISY

We're woken up to the sound of the bay doors opening. The loud metal-on-metal scraping noise sends chills up my spine. I've spent eighty-three cycles in the cage beside Meiko. We've been fed once a day and that's about it. We poop on the floor and they laser it away when they deliver our food. Meiko hates to release her bowels but I do it every single chance I get. Do I like having the smell assaulting my nostrils all day long? No, but I do it because I know holding it is not good for the human body. I can't afford to do stupid things that might make me sick when there's no medical care available.

I hate the layers of grime covering my skin. Since there is no dirt or dust on the ship, I have to face up to the fact that this is what my own body generates when left to its own devices. I smell gross and to be quite honest, I disgust myself.

Meiko seems totally oblivious to our filthy state. Then again, I've noticed personal hygiene is not at the top of her priority list. She's too busy kicking ass and taking names. Today she's sporting a huge bruise on the side of her face. I hate our captors as much as she does, but I gotta say she earned that bruise. The guy who came to laser out our poop leaned in a little too close and she nearly ripped one of his fins right off. It took two of the fish dudes to pull her off him. She just laughed like a madwoman when they beat her and threw her back into her cell.

That's the kind of thing that happens after years of being held in captivity. You not only go a little stir-crazy—which I'm feeling as well—but you also just get to the point that you don't really care if you die or not. We still talk and try to keep each other company, but I would be just as happy to not wake up each morning as continue to live this horrible nightmare that my life's become. I daydream about joining my family in the ever after. They were all so religious, but this experience made me lose my faith. Why would God let something like this happen to me? I've been a good, decent human being. I went to church with my family and even taught Sunday school for a summer.

Heck, I never went all the way with a guy. Well, if I'm being honest, that wasn't an active choice on my part. There were so few men on Earth after things went bad that I didn't really get a chance. Still, to my way of thinking that still means I've been living a good Christian life. Anyway, fat lot of good it did me. I still got abducted and enslaved. If there's a God up there either he's forgotten about me or he's got a strange sense of humor.

"Get the hell up, Daisy. There's something really strange going on today." The sharp tone and curse word tell me Meiko is seriously freaking out. Coming to my feet, I back all the way up as far from the sunlight streaming in through the bay doors as possible. I steal a glance sideways and Meiko presses her lips together in a firm line, shaking her head slightly. She wants me to be quiet.

Though they seem to be offloading cargo containers and might forget about us, I get a sick feeling in my gut that we're part of the cargo being sold. The thought of being sold fills me with dread. I know enough about the 'verse to understand that although we've been treated like animals, our next owner may be in the mood to eat us or use us to make little half-alien babies.

Something flips in my mind. Before I clearly understood that was a possibility cognitively, but now it has hit me on a bone-deep level of knowing. I can't explain the difference, but it feels so much more real and terrifying.

Staring out the bay doors, I see desert and aliens milling around. We seem to be at some kind of open-air market where ships just set down in a gigantic circle and pull their cargo right out to sell. That's when it occurs to me that we're actually in a large shuttle, not a ship. I guess that makes sense. They'd never be able to put a spaceship down into a marketplace like this.

For some reason, they're not coming to get us. Relief surges through my body and I almost go limp. Instead, I slide down to sit against the wall, making myself as inconspicuous as possible. Meiko follows my lead. We scoot together and whisper.

"I guess this isn't our last stop."

She huffs out an exasperated breath. "Just because they're not pulling us out to sell, doesn't mean we're not being sold. Maybe they've already sold us and are waiting for the buyer to arrive or something like that."

My anxiety spikes again. I whisper, "I don't want to be separated from you."

"If they open our cages for any reason, we need to fight like we've never fought before."

"I don't know how we could possibly win against them."

Her hand reaches through the bars and she grabs my wrist. "You have got to stop being such a good little victim and wake the fuck up, Daisy. There's no Prince Charming coming to rescue us. We've got to rescue ourselves or we're likely going to die an ugly and painful death. You've got to be able to see that by now."

My eyes fly from my wrist to her eyes. Is that what I'm doing? Pondering it for a brief second, I realize it's not that at all. Her dirty fist won't let go when I try to shake her off, so I stop trying. "I tried to fight them and it always ended the same way. They're bigger and stronger. They have weapons. I'm not about continuing to fight battles we never win."

"This time will be different. We'll fight together. Maybe we can get ahold of one of their weapons. You were in the military, so you know all about windows of opportunity. We're on a damned planet for the first time ever. Don't let this chance slip away."

I don't correct her that I was not actually in the military. Even I admit there's a subtle distinction between working for the government and being assigned to work with a military detachment and actually being in the military.

I nod without meaning to. She's right, of course. Even if it's only a one percent chance, we need to grab it. My wheels begin to turn, bringing my military training to the fore. "Our best chance will be when they least expect it. If we find ourselves in a situation with just one of them, we make our move. Drag him back behind the cages, where we're out of visual range of the others. Then we need to slip around and exit whichever side has the fewest crewmembers to notice."

A smile jumps onto her dirty face and her dark eyes

sparkle. "Finally, you're getting with the program. This is going to work. Trust me on that."

I honestly think my new friend just likes to fight, but then again that's what we need right now, a good fighter. If the look of determination in her eyes is any indication, maybe we'll kick ass and actually make our escape. I close my eyes and say a silent prayer.

When I open my eyes, something shifts in my psyche. "If ever there was a time to fight, it's now." Shooting her an anxious smile, I add, "I'm really not wild about the idea of becoming some alien's pet."

Just then one of our captors walks into the bay and pulls down a computer terminal from overhead. His fingers move across the keyboard and each of our cages begin to shimmer with a pink light. Goose bumps raise on my skin and it begins to itch slightly. Both Meiko and I come to our feet, trying to figure out what's going on.

It takes me a moment to realize the grime from Meiko's face and body seems to be lightening. At first I didn't notice because of the bruise, but the longer we stand there, the more obvious it becomes that we're becoming less and less dirty. "It's some kind of sonic shower. We're getting cleaner." Holding out my hand, I exclaim, "See, the dirt's going away." I begin to vigorously rub my skin. It helps the process, so I run my fingers through my hair as well, delighted to finally be clean after so long.

For some reason Meiko doesn't look nearly as elated as I do. Then it hits me like a ton of bricks. God, I'm so dumb. My uncle owned a used car lot before Earth went belly-up. Every Saturday morning we cleaned his cars so they'd be shiny enough to attract the notice of a buyer. Suddenly, I wish that I could put all the grime right back onto my skin. My hands drop to my sides as the bars of our cage pull back.

The top goes up and the side bars slide into the metal flooring.

A chill creeps up my spine. It's now or never time. Plastering a smile on my face as we step forward, I look for an opportunity to attack. This isn't the first time I've eyed them for physical weaknesses. I have no idea where their internal organs are or where they're vulnerable. Their fins are really sensitive but attacking them there usually just pisses them off. I decide his throat is a good option. Even if he breathes through his gills, damaging his throat will keep him from making noise and give us time to neutralize him. Sweet Jesus, I've never thought about how to keep a person from screaming while I killed them before. This is totally new territory for me but looking at his smirking face is helping me warm up to the idea.

We stop our approach, making him come closer to us. He's still smirking at us and I realize he's the one with the damaged fin, and he's admiring the unsightly bruise he left on Meiko's face. I look down, like a good little slave, wishing I had a nice big club to bash his head in with. I'm shocked at the brutality of my own thoughts.

My idea of hiding behind the cages turned out to be a bust, since the bars disappeared. We both pounce at the same time and I'm perversely thrilled by how shocked the foolish alien is. I'm guessing that he didn't see that coming. We hit his throat, punch his face and rip at his fins. He's flailing about, trying to fend us both off when there's a commotion at the bay door.

Two huge aliens with wings are literally gaping at us. Guess they never saw naked human girls have a throwdown. I don't let up on our guy but notice others of his kind rushing in to lend a hand. Suddenly, the large room is filled with more than a dozen aquatics. They begin grabbing at us and manhandling us. One of them punches me in the back, sending a jolt of pain down my spinal cord.

A roar splits the air and then all hell breaks loose. The two aliens with wings come bounding into the shuttle. Even though the vessel is huge, the floor shakes from the pounding of their massive booted feet. One of the aliens appears to be wearing a long skirt and the other a uniform. The one in the uniform pulls out two weapons and begins blasting every amphibian he can manage to get in his sights. A thought passes through my mind that I should be happy to see them finally get the comeuppance they so richly deserve. Instead I'm shocked that the winged alien is just indiscriminately killing them, like it's nothing to him.

The one wearing the skirt comes to a staggering stop in front of us, bends his knees and turns to join the fight. "Stay behind me, Queen Aiko. We will protect you with our lives."

My head jerks to look at Meiko and she mouths the word "sister." Before I can figure out what to do, she grabs me and pulls me down behind the guy. I see he's wearing billowing pants, not a skirt, but whatever. From what I can see the one we're hiding behind is roaring, hissing, and acting all kinds of threatening, but it's the other one who's doing all the killing. Maybe they're a fighting team and this is how they operate.

All I really know is the room stays lit up for endless minutes with laser fire. I slowly recognize the scent of burned flesh permeating the air and I gag a little. Just when I think it's going to die down, the exchange of fire picks up and the floor shakes again. I can't see what's going on, but it seems like more people joined the fight.

The guy shooting unfurls his wings in a gesture that seems protective, both for us and the guy standing in front. I realize they're absolutely amazing. His wingspan is huge. They keep snapping closed and then flaring about again as if he's trying to use them to seem larger than he is in an effort to intimidate his enemies even more. I can't imagine anything could be more intimidating to the aquatics than him killing a bunch of them.

His wings are gorgeous. They remind me of bat wings, except for the interesting coloration in muted blues and purples with a little amber thrown in for good measure. I keep catching glimpses of tattoos dancing down one side of his back. It's fanciful birds, dragons, and flying men with wings. One's tail is wrapped around a dragon egg. I know we should be paying attention to staying alive, but we can't do anything but crouch and hide until the battle is over.

A dark thought crosses my mind. If the victor gets the spoils, I guess that means we now belong to the dragon guys. Dragon guys? Where did that come from? Sighing, I realize it came from looking at the guy's tattoos. I wonder if they are dragon guys why they don't just shift into dragon form and take care of business. My thoughts circle back around to being owned by the dragon men, and I can't say that I find that idea very appealing.

The minute the weapons stop firing, I make a run for the bay door. My bare feet slip in black amphibian blood and I almost trip over one of the bodies. Skirting around half a dozen gaping dragon guys, I bound out the door.

For lack of better options Meiko follows me. Yep, we're running buck naked through the makeshift marketplace at breakneck speed. The problem is we have no idea where in the hell we're even going. We keep right on running though. My toes dig into the fine granules of sand and the hot golden sun beats down on my shoulders. It feels as though I'm being warmed from the inside out. After being cold for so long, I love it. A feeling of freedom ripples through my body and I know that I should stop and come up with a better plan than running into the desert, but I just can't make my feet stop moving.

The air around me moves and the two dragon guys from the shuttle drop down on either side of us. They don't speak. Instead they just run alongside of us, totally oblivious that we're actually trying to get away from them. After a few hundred yards, I look over at the big scarred one. He looks so serious with his chiseled jawline and big pointy horns.

"Where do we go, my queen? Are there other queens in need of rescuing?"

His voice is deep and rich. My girl parts sit up and pay attention, even as my feet slow down. Shooting Meiko a questioning look, we stop running. I try to be smooth. "Not that we know of. We just felt like running."

The pretty one speaks up, his tone respectful and humble. "Begging your pardon, gentle queens, but I was given to understand that human queens preferred walking rather than running and clothing as opposed to no clothing." Turning to Meiko, he dips his head. "You told me yourself that you never wished to be without clothing again, Queen Aiko."

We glance awkwardly at each other before Meiko speaks carefully chosen words. "Let me get this straight." Pointing to her chest with a thumb, she states. "My name is Aiko Hara and I'm your queen?"

Both males drop to one knee with their heads bowed. The good-looking one murmurs, "Forgive us for failing to show proper respect."

I'm the most confused that I've been in my lifetime. They think Meiko is her sister, who is their queen. My friend laughs. "Yes. Yes, I am your queen. I command that you get us clothing and something to eat." Making a gesture with one hand, she adds, "Quick. Quick. We don't want to get sunburned."

They come to their feet and the scarred one asks, "Where is your escort? I would recover their bodies rather than leave them on this barren world."

"We came by ourselves and got caught by the amphibians."

The handsome one's hand comes up to caress the bruise on her face. "You should never leave the ship without an escort. Even in the Naxis, human queens are precious. We have no wish to see you come to such harm again."

Meiko deadpans right back, "What an amazing coincidence. I have no wish to be harmed again. I wish to go back to our ship and be taken to my chambers, the chambers of Queen Aiko."

The big guy's face drops into a frown. "What other chamber would we place you in other than your own? You insisted upon choosing your own quarters and upon making the special shrine where you worship yourself."

Meiko immediately begins to tear up and it takes me a moment to realize her sister's set up a shrine probably to pray for her twin's safe return. I begin to tear up as well, because seeing my tough, belligerent friend in her moment of vulnerability is so bittersweet it breaks my heart. I rush over to her and give her a hug. It's kind of weird because we're not wearing clothing, but only a fool would worry about that now.

The scarred one speaks in a gruff tone. "Roan, you have made the queens leak. I do not understand. You are supposed to have experience with pleasing queens, yet they leak."

Meiko grips me tighter and laughs through her tears as the dragon guys continue to argue.

"I have experience with Draconian queens, not human queens. You know this, Darnok. Human queens are frail and they leak often. We must console them as best we can."

We don't even fight the two men when they draw us apart and tuck us under their wings. The scarred one called Darnok wraps one massive wing around me and gently holds me to his chest. I realize a couple of things immediately. He smells wonderful, like musk and old leather. Being under his wing should gross me out, but it feels amazingly warm and comfortable. Laying my head on his chest, I can hear a double thump where humans normally have a steady heartbeat.

Roan must have done the same for Meiko because she grows quiet for a time. I hear her dude saying soothing things to her. My guy tries to do that but it comes out all wrong. "Do not worry, my queen. We rent your enemies limb from limb. They can no longer force their will upon you."

Oh God, that's the straw that broke the camel's back so to speak. Both Meiko and I gape at the guy attempting to console me. At this point I can't be certain, but this feels like a rescue.

Meiko finally speaks. "I'm not Aiko." Her guy carefully unwraps her from his wing just a bit to give her space. She looks up at him, clearly nervous about telling him the truth. "My name is Meiko. I'm Aiko's twin sister. That shrine is probably for me, not her. You know, to pray for my safe return."

The large warrior jerks to attention. "You are newly freed queens?"

She nods. "The aquatics have a ship in space. I can't be

certain but I think we might not have been the only human females they abducted. Daisy and I fought them whenever they woke us up, so they stopped putting us back into hibernation."

The big handsome alien's hand came up again to her bruised face. "The males we killed gave you this damage?"

Nodding, she seems to be getting emotional again.

His fingers glide gently around the edges of the bruise on her face. "If I could, I would kill them all over again and make it more painful."

That's about the sweetest but strangest thing I've ever heard, and I think Meiko feels the same way. She steps back out from under his wing. "Don't worry about it. I made them bleed more than once. I may be small, but I'm mean as hell."

He folds his wings behind him and dips his head submissively. "Of course you did, my queen. How best may I serve you?"

Meiko is about as lost as I am. Frowning, she asks, "What kind of question is that?"

Shooting his companion a quick glance, he rephrases his question. "I wish to serve you in any way you wish. Ask anything of me and I will do my best to get it for you?"

Taking a step closer to him, I see her expression turn serious. "You really want to know what would best please me? What I want more than anything else in the entire universe right now?"

Nodding, he seems mesmerized by the tone of her voice.

"I want to see my sister, and then I want that aquatic ship disabled and boarded. Then I want every square inch of it searched and any women there freed. That's what would please me greatly."

Her big handsome rescuer swallows thickly. "Queens lead and males comply. That is the law."

Meiko states emphatically, "I'm not a queen."

"You are. All females are queens." His eyes trail up and down her naked body hungrily as tip of his tail reaches out to caress her calf. "You are more queenly than most human females. It is my honor to obey your commands."

My guy just holds me tighter and says absolutely nothing. I don't look at him because I'm not feeling whatever it is that's flowing back and forth between Meiko and her dragon man. Plus, there's that whole rending people limb from limb thing he mentioned. I know what he said is the plainly stated truth because I was there and saw it for myself.

However, talking about it didn't do much to endear him to me. I mumble quietly, "That's all great and wonderful, but I just want to be taken somewhere safe and be with the other human women."

Without a word, Darnok scoops me up into his arms and when his massive wings flap, we lift off the ground. I don't know where we're going exactly, but my stomach is doing flips. He flies so high up in the air that I can't even see the ground. Not that I try, because looking down will just make it worse. Instead, I close my eyes and feel the warm breeze in my face. This day has gone from horrible to bearable. Though I've still got no clothing and I'm starving, things are definitely looking up.

4 NO BREEDER

DARNOK

Watching Roan woo his queen is a stark reminder than I am no breeder. Where my attractive friend is bold and has a soothing voice, I am just the opposite. If there were any other warrior present, I would take my leave of the diminutive queen I rescued. Since there is none, I do my best to mimic Roan's interaction with his female.

My statement of rending the pretty queen's abductors limb from limb was met by a wide-eyed stare and her moving away from me slightly. Why I thought a queen would find comfort in such brutality is beyond my ability to reason at the moment. My hastily chosen words are proof in my own mind that I am not fit company for a queen.

We touch down near our shuttle as my team is loading the last of our medical supplies into the lower hold. We walk the females directly into the shuttle and strap them into seats. Roan fusses over his female, getting her a warm blanket to cover her nakedness. I rush to do the same for the one called Queen Daisy. She is named after a pretty flower from her home world. I know because the translator imbedded behind my ear draws forth images of white flowers.

In a way I am proud to be serving her for this brief moment in time. It is an honor that one such as me would never expect in his lifetime. I do not look her in the eyes or allow her to spend any amount of time gazing at my scarred-up face. Fortunately, my uniform covers most of my other scars. When I catch her looking at the ones on my hands as I cover her with the blanket, I press a food bar and hydration pouch into her hands and move quickly away. Subjecting a queen to my personage is not polite. Besides, I have a report to make to our commander about the aquatic ship in orbit.

Roan sits beside the queen he found favor with, and she seems to be doing better. He explains, "We will have your new shuttle up and running as soon as parts can be sourced. We left warriors on the ground to guard your property and begin making what repairs they can. It is a worthy vessel."

Another warrior sounds off. "I believe the enemy's transport vessel is the property of Queen Cassandra, for we were under her command when we stumbled upon these new queens needing rescue."

Roan frowns. "Queen Cassandra has many shuttles in her fleet. How can we deny these needy queens their own transportation?"

A third warrior joins the conversation. "I admit to being confused about this situation. We are not used to answering to multiple queens." Shooting me a quick glance he explains, "Before we came to this sector of space, there was only one queen per ship and each warrior had been specifically claimed so we knew who we answered to."

My friend is pensive for a long moment before speaking. "I believe we should answer to Queen Cassandra for our assignment, but respect our two new queens' wishes when it comes to the shuttle that was taken in battle, since we fought on their behalf."

Meiko speaks up, motioning to Queen Daisy with one hand. "We'll make it simple for you by laying claim to the shuttle and that amphibian ship in orbit. I demand you secure the vessel for me and kill those filthy slave traders."

The men all jerk to attention. It's because not only did Meiko issue a direct order usurping our current leader's command, but because they're also eager for a glorious battle to rescue more women. It's the dream of every warrior to serve a queen and more queens mean a better chance of being selected.

Meiko states emphatically, "If Miss Cassandra has a problem with any of that she can come and talk to me about it."

The warriors shoot each other anxious glances. Worry niggles at the back of my mind as well because it sounds like Queen Meiko intends to challenge our queen. Though males have no right to interfere in queenly affairs, I find myself reluctant to follow this new queen. Queen Cassandra has proven herself, and her rule gives us a stability we've not known before. I steal a quick glance at Queen Daisy and find her lost in her own thoughts with her drink halfway to her pretty little mouth. Reaching out, I encourage her to hydrate.

She complies without making a fuss. Something in my chest loosens to have a queen so effortlessly do my bidding. It makes me feel powerful and protective both at the same time. My fist comes to my chest to rub away this strange new feeling. I move to the front of the shuttle to use the communications array. We lift off as I attempt to give a report to Mathadar on this situation.

There is no aquatic vessel in orbit. Since queens would

never lie, that means they are using some other type of ship. Mathadar agrees to scan for aquatic life signs and for human queens. Perhaps these two are the only ones in need of rescue today, but we must to be certain before we leave this area.

Dropping down into a chair, it groans under my weight. We are in the Naxis now. The aquatics should be closed off in Exion space, yet they are here. It occurs to me to wish we had not killed them all, for questioning one might yield much useful information. I wish to know why they are here and under whose authority they continue to enslave human queens. Those are questions I will have answers to before we break orbit.

Looking back at Queen Daisy, my heart stutters in my chest to see her sitting all alone, looking vulnerable and forlorn. Perhaps she believes she is moving from the control of one set of unjust males to the hands of another. She needs a male to console her, like Roan consoles her friend. I am not fit for such a task, yet I do not wish to assign another to take her under his wing. She fit nicely under my wing earlier and it grieves me deeply to be such a misfit.

Queens Cassandra and Aiko are waiting for us. They step over the threshold the moment the loading bay depressurizes. The twin queens look so much alike that I cannot tell them apart. They rush to one another and hug as Queen Meiko awkwardly clutches her wrap around her shoulders. Seeing the sheer joy on their faces is enough to brighten a day filled with death and destruction. Roan sweeps them away, one under each wing.

I attempt to give a more detailed verbal report to Takadon Mathadar even as Queen Cassandra approaches the frail queen and begins to put her at ease. Her delicate features slowly relax but she remains suspicious of her surroundings.

"Darnok, I need your full attention. The lives of queens may be at risk."

Tearing my eyes away from Queen Daisy, I apologize. "I beg your forgiveness, Commander. After seeing her so ruthlessly attacked, I worry over our new queen."

"As well you should. I never disliked aquatics in particular until they began this new business of abusing queens."

Nodding, images rise in my mind of the pure blind rage that overtook my better judgment when I saw the naked queens being harmed. "You will be pleased to know that Roan fought like a demon to rescue the queens, protecting them with his own body."

Mathadar's expression shifts from annoyance to one of amusement. "Unless I am much mistaken, you likely tripled his kill rate."

I know exactly what he is insinuating. "Breeders have more heart than skill in battle, that much is true. Still, he stepped up without hesitation when queens needed protecting. For that I am relieved and proud of my friend."

My commander's wings lift slightly. "As am I, Darnok. It was good that he was at your side this day. Having a breeder on hand to initiate the care of abused queens is desirable. I will ensure one is added to all away teams moving forward."

Pleased with Mathadar's praise of my friend and his plan to integrate breeders in the future, I am well satisfied with the success of our mission. Since I wish to attack the aquatics and search for more human queens, I ask, "What did our scans reveal?"

"There is an older ship in orbit with a mixture of alien

species, including aquatics. They are holding almost a hundred queens in what we believe to be hibernation chambers situated along the entire underbelly of their ship. The queens are stationary and their respiration is suppressed. It is an area unsuitable for the placement of anything but cargo."

"A hundred humans?" Anger flares in my gut. My mind can barely fathom such a number of small queens being abused.

Mathadar clutches the data pad in his hand. "I am told one hundred is considered a trading unit in this sector of space. Since they consider the females cargo, this makes perfect sense."

"We've put a stop to their trade in human slaves several times now. Why do they persist in believing they can get away with this kind of crime?"

"Our other battles have been in the Exion sector. Our last battle resulted in the tear in space being closed off between the Naxis and Exion sectors. We believe they are merely stranded in this sector with the queens they intended to take back to Exion."

"Queen Cassandra told us that all beings are free in this sector." My chest aches from the thought of what those queens are going through. Truth be told, my trigger finger is also aching to blast the criminals to oblivion.

"It is true that the aliens in this sector of space are unforgiving of such transgressions. It is interesting that the amphibians took only the two queens who were not being held in hibernation. My best guess is they wanted rid of them because even long-range scans can pick up breathing queens. Even now they are slowly covering the exterior of their ship in a special mineral. It is making it difficult to continue monitoring the suppressed life signs of the hibernating queens. I can only guess this is an attempt to avoid being detected as they try to find a way back to their sector of space."

"I will not allow that to happen. The rescued queens have tasked us with disabling that ship and freeing any queens we find confined there. They wish to take possession of that ship."

"Queen Cassandra was livid at the thought of so many of her kind being enslaved. She commands us to rescue them as well. This ship is of little value. If the new queens wish to have it, they will be responsible for its upkeep."

"Roan and I will stay on board and ensure it is space worthy."

"Agreed. We are fortunate that your team found the queens on the planet below. If not for that stroke of good luck, I feel certain they would have succeeded in keeping the queens hidden away in their hold."

"Since I do not have skills flying a fighter, I wish to be part of the boarding party."

"Consider it done. Report to bay nine upon your arrival. That is where the planning is taking place. I will message them to expect you."

Dipping my head, I murmur, "I wish only to serve, Takadon Mathadar."

"As do we all, Darnok. Go and enjoy the coming battle. Lovely queens who have never known our kind are waiting to be rescued."

My bloodlust rushes to the fore and I run to meet my fate. Visions of the beautiful queen who sheltered a moment under my wing float through my mind. Her soft body pressed against mine was a privilege I never expected to enjoy. Now, she is all I can think of, her pretty eyes and long pale strands. Never in all my life have I set eyes on a more beautiful queen. Now, I must ensure no more harm comes to her fellow queens.

5 HELPING HANDS

DAISY

I've been greeted by the other women and assigned a tiny resting space with a door that locks. The two warriors who rescued us are busy carrying out Meiko's commands to search the amphibian ship for other women and commandeer it for us. I'm a little lost about why they just seem to do whatever we say, and it blows my mind that we're going to own the very ship they kept us enslaved on. That's the kind of poetic justice that only happens in science fiction movies and such.

Looking around the neat, clean space, I have to admit that it sure sounds like all my wildest fantasies have come true. First a hot dragon warrior has a big throwdown with the asshats that abducted me and pretty much wipes the floor with the miserable freaks. Then I get to live on a ship with a bunch of other human women. The icing on the cake is that the crewmembers will be all male, and if I understand this correctly, they worship women like actual queens. Looking down at the long flowing gown drives home the fact that everything's all upside down. Who in the heck wears a gown on a spaceship? Sighing, I guess that would be me.

I head out of my tiny room and walk down the hall to the dining area. Slipping in unnoticed, I grab a piece of fruit and a hydration package and look around for a quiet corner.

It sounds kind of cockamamie when I string it all together in my mind, but it's true nonetheless. I can tell the other women have all been through something, because they're a little standoffish with the men and cling together in little groups. It's almost like they don't trust their turn of good fortune to not swing abruptly in the opposite direction.

To be honest, I know the feeling quite well. This whole situation has that too-good-to-be-real quality about it. Being locked in a cage for over a year as well as in and out of hibernation for God knows how long... well, it changes a person. After getting smacked down by our captors that last time, I know deep down inside that my personal power is not enough to keep me safe out in the black of space. If the dragon warriors, who I now know are called Draconians, hadn't come to our rescue, the amphibians would have beat the crap out of us and put us right back in that cage or sold us to some unscrupulous alien who thinks it okay to own people.

Anyway, I've decided to hang back and simply observe, watching for cracks in the façade they present to us every minute of every day. That's why I choose to sit alone at a corner table in the dining hall. The whole setup in here is a little strange to me. The tables and chairs hover. The odd part is how nothing falls off. There's just this gentle bob that you hardly notice. If I'm being honest, it makes sitting for long periods of time easier. So I sit, trying to take everything in without seeming like I'm gawking at folks.

Want to know the only woman here who seems to be laughing it up? That would be my friend Meiko. During our months together, the fate of her missing twin was the only conversation she refused to have with me. I assumed her refusal to talk, coupled with her extreme level of aggressiveness with our abductors, meant she'd watched her sister die or something equally awful. It turns out the unbearable pain of losing that close connection to her sister was slowly killing her on the inside. Even though I was in the cage right next to hers, I can't imagine what that must have been like for her. She kept her emotions about that hidden.

She's sure not doing that anymore. Both Meiko and her twin sister are happy as clams. Although her sister is a little more reserved, I think it's because she's meaner. I know that sounds awful to say and God forgive me, but it's true. She orders the other women around and she has all the warriors hopping. I'd be embarrassed to act that way, but she sees no wrong in it. I don't want to get bossed around by her, so I try to maintain a distance.

When Meiko catches my eye and begins to walk over with her sister in tow, I know that avoidance is not going to be my primary play today. I love that my friend is ridiculously happy. Heck, any of us would give our right arm to have family with us, especially with things going so badly on Earth. She's got that and the thing is, Meiko fully realizes how lucky she is.

Plopping down on the seat across from me, she picks up a cracker from my plate and crams it in her mouth. Barely taking time to chew, she speaks. "Hey Daisy, I've been looking for you."

"Lucky girl, you found little ol' me."

"Are you as bored as we are?"

Now that sounds like a setup, but I answer her truthfully. "Some women have crew jobs but they didn't think I was quite ready for that." I smooth down the front of my pretty blue gown and try not to be indignant about it. "Maybe I'm not ready, since I'm doing the lone wolf thing." God, I'm pathetic.

"Guess what Roan told me?"

Waggling my eyebrows, I tease, "One can only imagine what that gorgeous hunk whispered in your ear."

Laughing, she shakes her head sending wisps of dark hair flying. "That ship we were on has almost a hundred humans, all women. Cassandra scanned it and discovered the aquatics have them squirreled away in hibernation tanks."

Shock rolls through my body. "I never thought there were so many of us." Feeling my rage boiling over, I clinch my fists.

Leaning forward, she whispers, "Some of the bio signs are smaller and weaker. We think they might be kids."

Coming to my feet, I feel like I'm going to throw up. "Children? Did you say they've abducted children?"

Standing, she grabs my arm to steady me. "I said kids but yeah, that's what I meant."

Her sister speaks up. "The breeders are going to set up one of the bays as a receiving center with warm blankets, showers, and hydration packs. Kind of like an emergency triage site."

I don't like that she called them breeders. It seems awfully disrespectful, since Roan is one and he killed, maimed, and risked his own life to set us free. Glancing over her shoulder at the woman who looks just like her, Meiko murmurs, "We're going to help them take care of the rescues."

My chest loosens as I realize there's hope for the

women. Forcing my nausea away, I get with the program. "Seeing a friendly face might help keep them calm, and we can advocate for them in case things get sticky. I want to help.

Pulling me along behind her, we head for the door. "That's why I came looking for you, girl. Let's get a move on."

The moment we slide into the emergency center they've set up, Roan notices. God, he looks like garbage. He's got a large cut along his right temple, his lip is split, and he has a huge darkened area along his right side. I'm guessing that's what a bruise looks like on one of them. We're too late to help with setup, because there is already about thirty of them in the bay. Several caretakers seem to be directing a small contingent of warriors in caring for them. I'm guessing Roan and these warriors brought over the first batch because the warriors are looking kind of rough as well.

His eyes shift from Aiko to Meiko and then grow heated as a smile tugs at the corners of his mouth. He glances back down to the woman he's tending to. She's an older woman who appears weak. He's helping her drink from a hydration packet by lifting her head slightly and holding the packet to her lips. We watch her nod and sit the rest of the way up while taking the packet from him. He tugs a blanket around her before standing to greet us.

We jog over and Meiko slips under his wing, giving him a little hug. I can't say I'm surprised that she's taken a liking to the big handsome man. They're so wrapped up in staring into each other's eyes that Aiko snaps her fingers in front of their faces. "Come on, love birds. We've got work to do."

Roan shoots her a disgruntled look but steps back, releasing Meiko. "The healers are performing a triage, taking the most physically damaged queens to the healing units for treatment."

He motions to several males with the green piping on their uniforms that I've come to associate with medical personnel. They've set up half a dozen healing platforms the size of small beds, each with an occupant. The platforms hover off the floor about three feet and are attached to some kind of computer console that appears really high-tech.

Roan continues, "We've broken apart the other duties and we are responsible for greeting queens after they've been medically scanned. The healers need information on their prior medical issues."

Before we can respond there is a shocking impact to the ship and the floor sways under our feet. We grab onto each other, trying to quell our panic, but Roan just grins mischievously. "I guess some folks don't want to give up the rest of their stolen queens today."

"Oh my God, we're fighting the other ship." I imagine huge bolts of laser fire hitting our ship. Since I saw the damage their small laser pistols cause, I can't imagine us surviving a huge cannon-size laser blast. Sucking in breath after breath, I feel myself becoming lightheaded as images flash through my mind of a huge hole being torn into the ship and our bodies getting sucked into outer space.

A hand comes out hard and fast around my upper arm and Aiko's annoyed voice sounds off. "Get yourself together or get the hell out. Ain't nobody here got time to baby your ass."

You would think that might spark my anger, but it's nowhere to be found. I feel broken and like I've lost something critical to my being. Once again someone else has to step in and defend me. Since Draconian males would burn in hell before they contradicted a queen, Meiko speaks up.

"Put a cork in it, Aiko. If we've got an ounce of compassion for the women being rescued today, then we'll make time to support the ones who got rescued yesterday."

Aiko looks taken aback and stammers, "I didn't mean anything by that."

"I know. I like how we give each other a swift kick in the pants, but Daisy doesn't know that's what you're doing. She probably thinks you're serious."

"I am serious about us needing to pull our shit together to help the women who come rolling in here. They're going to be a hot mess. Still, I get what you're saying about treating your friend like we treat each other."

After hearing them talk it out, I feel better. "It's fine. Aiko's right. I need to feel useful again. This is the perfect way for me to contribute. I guess the abuse is still pretty fresh for me."

Roan interjects kindly, "If it is any source of consolation, Darnok is continuing the assault aboard the enemy vessel and has vowed to leave no aquatic standing."

I know better than to think he's just planning to cut off their legs, because I saw what he did to the ones down on the planet when he rescued me. Call me odd, but I'm not as thrilled as Roan is that his friend is killing a bunch of bad guys. Also, Darnok seems like a relatively decent guy. I hate that he's risking his life all over again. From the look of him, he's been in a fight or two and I'm worried he's going to step into one too many and wind up dead.

Meiko's got other ideas on that subject. "I'm glad he's vowed to kill them all. If we leave the fuckers roaming around, they're just going to keep doing what they're doing. I don't want any other women thrown in a cage by them."

I sigh to myself, because she ain't wrong about that. I hate to judge all the aquatics by the ones we had contact with, because our caretakers were real assholes. I can well imagine them continuing to do exactly what they're doing. "I guess you're right. Let's face facts; it takes quite a bit of time and effort to abduct a hundred women. My gut tells me they ain't gonna stop until someone stops them."

Aiko lights up. "Darnok is definitely the man for the job. Come on and let's start gathering background information on the rescues. It's already getting crowded, but it's going to be a madhouse in here very soon."

I nod. "Show me what to do."

Roan pulls over a hover board and begins unloading food bars and hydration packets. We're given data pads and drift apart to begin interviews. Even though my hands are moving and I'm getting things done, my mind is a million miles away on the big scarred-up warrior who put himself between me and danger. I give a silent prayer that he's okay and ask God to protect him. Does God protect aliens? I have to think he does. We're all his children after all. No matter where in the 'verse we're born or hatched, I feel He's watching over us. I know they all have their own gods, but in this moment I honestly believe we're all talking about the same God, only in different ways.

6 BATTLE SCARRED

DARNOK

We attach a grappling hook to the door of the only loading bay on the enemy ship. It's an older ship but appears to be well constructed. This explains why it takes a blast from our laser cannons and three firm jerks with the grappling hook to pull the cursed door off. Once our ship has removed the door and it is drifting away under its own momentum from being removed from the door casing, we land our shuttles quickly and disembark.

Meeting heavy resistance is not an unexpected scenario. Their best chance of turning us back is when we first arrive. We're seasoned warriors. Not only can we anticipate their tactics, we're prepared to brutally push forward in search of the hibernating queens. Within moments, the huge bay is thick with smoke from our laser pistols.

I spread my wings and take to the air. Seeing more of the enemy swarm into the far side of the room, I toss an explosive device and watch with satisfaction as it rips through their flesh, sending them sprawling in every direction.

Pushing through the door with several warriors at my

back, we leave the remaining crew to finish the battle. Roan is with them. I wish he were with me. Though he is holding his own, his fighting skills are not the best.

A worry niggles in the back of my mind. These creatures are without honor. That makes them both self-serving and unpredictable. Such beings may attempt to dispose of the queens. Though I can't imagine it happening in this particular situation, we should waste no time getting to the lower levels in order to protect them from such unspeakable violence.

We rampage through the ship, destroying everything in our path. As we get closer to the lower levels, our enemy thins out. By the time we reach the door leading down to the lower hold, we are sweaty and covered in dark alien blood. I have felt the lasers burn through my flesh, not once but twice, yet I press onward. One face drives me. It is fair Queen Daisy's sad visage. Perhaps if I save enough of her fellow queens, it will put a smile on her lovely face.

We place incendiary devices at the door and step back. It's a crude but effective way to force entry. We back away in order to set the charge off and my comm unit comes to life.

"Darnok, it's Roan. We fought our way to the third level and discovered a medical bay filled with many queens. They have them shielded from our scans in a large cube. We are deactivating it now."

"Are the queens well?"

"These queens appear to be older or damaged. Several have white hair and others are missing limbs or sickly. I'm getting them back to our ship until the battle is over and repairs to this vessel can be made."

"Good job, my friend. Protect the queens at all costs."

As the charge detonates, destroying the door, I am still

reeling at the fact that there are apparently one hundred and thirty queens aboard this vessel. When the dust clears, what we see when we enter the huge room steals my breath away. There are many tall glass cylinders and they each contain a queen. A few are pounding on the glass, but mostly appear to be in an endless sleep. Though the furious queens have no words, I know they are demanding to be set free. These humans are not amphibian, so the devices strapped onto their faces must be delivering breathable air. They dare not pull them off and neither do we.

The few amphibians standing around do not have weapons, but I am still sorely tempted to kill them. Yes. I dislike these males most of all, for they are tasked with controlling and abusing the queens. Slowly drawing my laser pistol one last time, I point it at the nearest of them. "The angry queens wish to be released. You will comply with all their orders from this point forward."

He stammers, "We do not have enough cages to house them properly."

My finger has a mind of its own. Before I can formulate a plan of action in my mind, the offending alien is dead. I casually turn my weapon on the next nearest of their crew. "Release the angry queens. Do it now."

Rather than arguing the logistics of removing them from their hibernation chambers, he runs to the nearest unit with an awakened queen and begins the process of freeing her. The moment the front of the unit swings open, she bolts forward. I am somehow not surprised that the very first thing she does is claw a bloody trail across the aquatic's face with her nails. Laughter sounds off from our crew. When she turns to glare at us, we drop submissively down onto one knee. I speak, trying to keep my voice humble. "We live to serve, my queen."

She's suspicious of our motivation and I can't say she is wrong to be such. "Why are you here?"

"Our human queen has tasked us with rescuing her sister queens. She commands that you be brought to our ship, for she was once a hostage of the same amphibians who enslaved you."

"Proceed. Make sure these crazy fucks are careful when they take the women out of the units. Coming out of the drug-induced stupor can be traumatic."

One of our males steps forward with a large cloth they have dug up from somewhere. She stares wide-eyed as he gently wraps it around her. He says soothing things to her, but I take her words to heart.

Getting on the communications unit, I contact Takadon Mathadar who will surely be at Queen Cassandra's side. His voice is tight with anxiety when he answers. "How goes the battle, Darnok?"

"We have found the multitude of queens, Mathadar. In addition to the hundred we picked up on our scan, there were still more queens being held in a medical bay. It looks like the count so far is one hundred and thirty."

He makes a sound of disbelief and excitement. I hear Queen Cassandra cheering.

Reading out messages from the other warriors, I assure him, "The ship is now secure. Even now warriors are clearing out the last of the aquatics."

"This is good news. Are the queens all alive and accounted for? Our scans couldn't lock on with so much laser fire and the minerals covering part of the outer hull."

"Their hibernation pods are all intact. We are taking the ones out that are awake, but many are drugged. We have been advised by the first queen we freed that sometimes the queens are traumatized by being released from the hibernation chambers. I request than you send our healers and more warriors to ease their transition to the shuttles."

Queen Cassandra's voice is the one that responds. "We will send healers and breeders right away. Get the ones out that are active and wait for reinforcements before removing the rest. We'll consider this an extraction."

Her words make sense to me. I know Queen Aiko wishes to claim this ship, but I am compelled to ask the question bearing on everyone's mind. "Will you wish to add this ship to your armada, my queen? If so we can begin making repairs right away."

"Believe it or not, the twins would like their own ship. They intend to fly with us, so I guess we're keeping the old bucket of bolts for now."

Glancing back out to the corridor, I see wires hanging out of the walls and a dead body lying on the floor. This place is probably in much worse condition than any of them realize. Trying to be accommodating, I respond positively. "It will take some time, but I believe this ship would be an asset to our people."

"Yeah, this one will make four, but what we really need is a home world."

This I well know. We now have well over two thousand warriors and too many frail queens to count. We need a pristine new world to call home, where we can build a city with safe barricades to protect our new queens and the families they enable us to have. Though I will never be lucky enough to breed, just knowing my brethren will spawn is enough to make my heart sing with joy.

We carefully supervise the amphibian biologists, ensuring they do not get near the queens except to remove the ones who are awake. It is a tedious job and we've removed most of them and ferried them to our vessel by the time our reinforcements arrive.

There are twenty warriors, a handful of breeders, and three human queens. One I recognize immediately. Daisy is with the twin queens and Roan. They come to me at once. I glance away when I see Queen Daisy's face contort into a mask of horror when her eyes slide over me.

For some reason her disapproval stings. Does she not know those of us who have seen many battles tend to collect scars? I immediately I remind myself that of course she has no knowledge of such things, for she is an innocent queen.

Suddenly, her hands are all over me. To my surprise, she's dabbing at my injuries with a clean cloth. My eyes fly up to Roan's and he smirks. "You got yourself some serious laser burn, Darnok. What happened to your personal shield?"

"It malfunctioned." Gazing at his many cuts and bruises, I grin. "You look like a warrior who saved thirty queens this day, my friend."

He preens a bit, clearly proud of his accomplishment. Before I can say more, Queen Daisy puts two fingers in her mouth and makes a loud high-pitched noise that has everyone turning to look at us. She shouts, "Medic, over here. We have an injured soldier."

I'm fascinated at her quick and efficient speech pattern and that she calls me by the name her people use for warrior. They are called soldiers. I know this because my language processor is pulling up images of both human males and females wearing body armor and carrying large weapons. I can't stop staring as she rips the seam apart from the arm of my uniform and carefully checks over my flesh.

It is beyond my comprehension to reason why she is so worried about one such as myself. I murmur, "Warriors are designed to take damage. This is nothing. It will heal without wasting precious resources."

Shaking her head, she pays no attention to my words. A confused healer meanders over with his medical kit. "Are you well, Darnok?"

"Of freakin' course he's not well. He's got wounds large enough for me to stick my fist in. Use one of your fancy gadgets and heal him." When the healer does not move quick enough to suit her, she commands, "Now."

The healer snaps out of it and whips out a dermal healing unit. Dialing the setting to its highest level, he begins running it over my skin. "There are queens here that need my attention. I should not be wasting time on a warrior."

Out comes one delicate little finger and she pokes him squarely in the chest. "Don't talk to him that way. He's a hero who risked his life to save women and got himself shot up for his trouble. You're supposed to care about people. Well guess what, warriors are people."

The healer stretches in frustration and his horns slip back. "Your will be done, my queen." He's thoroughly confused about why she's so intent on having my wounds healed. It's unnecessary, but she will not see reason on this particular issue. It makes something warm bloom in my chest.

Unlike the healer, I'm thrilled that she's protective of warriors. I feel the warmth unfurling in my chest double and then triple. My tail whips back and forth happily behind me. I like that she hangs over his shoulder, inspecting his work, and pointing out all the tiny spots he neglects.

When there is nothing but freshly healed skin, she motions him away. If I'd thought she was going to move on,

I'd have been very wrong. Instead she runs her soft hands over my skin, inspecting every bit of my arm before moving her hands over my chest. She still seems to be searching for injuries, but my body doesn't know that. Though we are in a crowded place and this caring queen is showing no signs of wishing to mate, my cock hardens anyhow. I can feel my mating scent rising and if she does not stop touching me soon, it will soon crest.

Moving my hands up to cover hers, I still her hands and then step back out of her reach. She twirls around, giving me her back, and I know the moment we shared is over. Turning on my heel, I stand back to back with her. My emotions are a jumbled mess and I must force my feet to move in order to put some distance between us.

The last thing I need is for her gesture of kindness to be met with lustful thoughts. That is no way to thank her for her kind concern for my well-being. Yet, I can scarcely help myself. I give my head one firm shake as if to dislodge all thoughts of the lovely queen and get on with overseeing the mission.

No matter where I move in this cavernous room, I maintain an awareness of where Queen Daisy is and what she is doing. My head is filled images of her walking in her flowing gown, handing out drinks, and speaking to the new human queens. She is quiet and sweet. They calm down when she speaks to them. It may be the same for the twin queens, but I do not watch them like I do Daisy.

I do not believe her gowns are nice enough to suit her lovely form. She needs fattening up a bit as well. Being so fresh from her ordeal with the aquatics, she has not had a chance to gain her normal weight back. I vow to see to that, thinking to send her gifts of fine foods fit to tempt the lovely queen's stomach.

I jerk back in wonder at myself for making plans in regard to this nice queen. She has not selected me for her protector, yet I act as though supporting her is my job. Just because she worried for my health one day does not mean she will wish me to approach her or try to care for her needs. The knowledge that she does not want me feels like a punch to the gut. I bear it because such is the truth.

Unfortunately, I have a stubborn disposition and therefore cannot leave the idea alone. In the final analysis I decide to simply care for her from afar. She does not need to know who provides for her needs after all. Worshiping a queen from afar is a time-honored tradition among my people. Draconian queens were few and expected the many warriors under her command to dote upon her, anticipating her every need. Human queens are no less worthy of love and devotion. My mind automatically corrects that last thought to be *obedience* and devotion.

7 HANDS ON A QUEEN

DAISY

Aiko's annoyance at Cassandra's decision to split the women up is evident. In an attempt to keep all of her eggs out of one basket our fearless leader distributed them evenly throughout the armada. That way we don't lose all the women in one fell swoop if they take out the ship housing them all. From my perspective it makes good sense, but Aiko has other ideas.

Since we were given possession of the ship we won in battle, I gotta say, it's mostly Aiko running the show around here with her sister backing her up. I'm kind of a third wheel, though I think of myself as a silent partner.

Cassandra sent an accompaniment of warriors, all volunteers from what I was told. Roan and Darnok are among the five hundred or so males that even now are crawling all over the ship cleaning up after the battle and making repairs. We're doing our share, but since we aren't mechanics, they've tasked us with small, time-consuming busy work to free up the warriors to make more important repairs.

It took the better part of a day for the five aquatic biologists to remove all the new women from their hibernation cylinders. Including the queens that were already on board, we have something in the neighborhood of a hundred and eighty women spread across the four ships containing roughly twenty-five-hundred warriors. There is some concern that it's not enough to keep the ships flying and protected.

Aiko's annoyed voice draws me from my internal musings. "I don't like it. We should keep all the women on the *Delacroy* with Tela. That ship has the best shields. Plus we can all work together to protect it." Aiko's been pretty cranky lately but she does keep working steadily as she gripes. Our black uniforms are smeared with the bright green transfer fluid that acts as a conductor between the fuel rods and the relays we're fitting them into.

Meiko shrugs. "We're not in charge, so it's not our decision to make."

"Yeah, I know." Blowing into the end of the fuel rod, she shakes it to see if it's still got a charge. It makes a little splashing noise if there's still fuel in the rod. She smiles and slips it back into place. "Twelve down and eight hundred and fifty-seven to go."

Checking all the small fuel rods in our communications array is tedious and boring. "I like feeling useful, so I don't mind repetitive tasks."

Meiko teases, "I'll bet Commander Darnok would love to assign you some repetitive tasks."

My head jerks up to stare at her. Her expression is filled with mischief. My face begins to heat, under her and her sister's gaze. "Shut up. You know he's not like that."

Aiko laughs, moving on to the next fuel rod. "Every guy is like that, even the alien ones."

Totally ignoring her comment, Aiko's makes it abundantly clear that she has a different warrior in her bed every night. Opening a new case of rods, I sift through them and begin pulling out the exact size we need for this job. "Well, Darnok doesn't want anything to do with me. The man won't even look in my direction."

"What do you expect? You gave him a boner in front of everyone. That's got to be humiliating?"

My eyes jump up to Meiko, who's staring at me intently. She shakes her head. "You didn't know that, did you?"

I realize my mouth is hanging open like the great big fool I am. Closing my eyes, I know the exact moment it happened. I was so preoccupied with checking him for injuries, that I accidentally got a little handsy. It was all kinds of awkward when he took my hands off his body. It seemed at the time like I'd transgressed some social rule, so I didn't think much of it.

"Well, I'm sorry if that was humiliating for him. I gotta say it was all kinds of embarrassing for me as well. Maybe I should apologize to him for overstepping my boundaries."

Meiko stops fidgeting with one of the rods and looks back at me. "You have got to be kidding. Do tell, how are you going to start that conversation?"

Aiko chimes in with a solicitous wag of her eyebrows, "It's not like you can say sorry for making his dick hard or anything like that. Anything less direct and the poor man is probably not going to understand what you're trying to say."

Smiling brightly, I focus on getting her to back off. "Gee, when we first met I thought you were kind of an asshat." She doesn't seem upset. "Now I can see you just have a bizarre sense of humor."

Meiko perks up. "I told you my sister would grow on you if you gave her a hot minute."

Holding out a brand-spanking-new mini fuel rod

between my thumb and index finger, I grumble. "Yep, she's growing on me all right, like a strange fungus. Too bad I'm a linguist and not a biologist or I might be enjoying it more."

Aiko frowns, snatching the fuel rod from my hand. "You're a big geek. I hope you know that."

"Yeah, unfortunately I do know that. I may have majored in linguistics but I minored in social awkwardness."

Laughing, Aiko deadpans back, "I can easily believe it. So what's your plan for the future? Are you going to snag a hot warrior and have a bunch of little dragon babies or delve into alien languages?"

"Well, those things are not mutually exclusive. You gotta admit that snagging a hot warrior seems like the best of some piss-poor options to me, so yeah, I'm gonna go with that plan."

Meiko sits on a console, swinging her legs carelessly. "Anyone capture your notice?"

"I'm going to take my time looking. How about you? You seem pretty comfortable under Roan's wing."

Aiko slides from around the console she's working on to grab a hydration packet. "Roan's all wrong for Meiko. She needs a fit warrior, not some huge ungainly breeder."

Meiko reaches over when she isn't paying attention and quickly squeezes her drink pouch, squirting a big gulp unexpectedly into Aiko's mouth. Aiko jerks back and tries to swallow, choking a bit in the process. Meiko takes advantage of the moment to put her sister in her place on the subject. "I don't need your seal of approval, sis. Roan's really protective, funny, sweet, and great in bed. If things keep going well, I'm probably going to keep him."

My mouth drops open in astonishment. "Wow, that was fast."

She has the decency to look sheepish. "We haven't known each other long, but I feel connected to him."

Aiko's disapproving voice interjects, "If you're going to keep him, you might as well be honest to yourself about why." Meiko turns to stare at her intrusive sister. Before she can speak, Aiko begins complaining. "I think you're getting attached to his little ones. God knows they're cute as hell, flying all around looking like demonic cherubs." Aiko's voice softens, "But you can't marry the dad just to get the babies."

My friend shrugs. "Don't act like you know me. Trust me, you don't."

Aiko laughs, "I know you better than you know yourself. I've had a damn lifetime to study your every move."

Though that sounds vaguely threatening to my ears, Meiko just laughs and throws her cleaning rag in Aiko's face. It was getting tense there for a minute with the two of them, but they're back to laughing it up again now. How do they even do that?

Truth be told, I'm a little envious of the two of them. It'd sure be nice to have someone I felt that close to. Meiko has it made in my opinion. She's got her twin sister and Mr. Tall, Dark, and Gorgeous looking out for her. Me on the other hand, I've got nothin' and nobody keeping up with me.

Suddenly, a drone comes whizzing into the bay. It's got a package. I jump to my feet and approach, because they're programmed to give supplies to whoever approaches. I think it's got to be more of those tiny fuel rods that we're quickly running out of on this job.

The drone drops down right in front of my eyes and I reach up, sliding the box out of the weird metal clamps the bot uses for hands. Turning I trot over, gingerly put the box on the console, and begin unsealing the top. Meiko and her sister don't even look over to see what I'm doing. They're still wrapped up in a conversation about Roan's little ones.

When I lift off the top, I'm stunned. Inside is an absolutely beautiful gown and matching shoes. The delicate fabric with tiny beaded trim calls to me, but I don't dare touch it. I recognize a courting gift when I see one and there ain't no guy on this ship tryin' to court me.

I know, wearing a gown in space seems absurd, but all the women have been getting them from the dragon warriors hoping to capture their attention. I haven't gotten any though, probably because I'm smaller than the other women. The warriors all seem to avoid me and are really careful when they have to interact with me. They swarm over the few larger women like they're the only ones fit to mate with. It sucks but there's nothing I can do about it. I'm not sure I want any of them to be interested in me anyway.

Turning to look over my shoulder, I shout, "Meiko, you have a drone delivery. It looks like a courting gift from your hot Draconian boyfriend." I know everyone calls them breeders but I just can't call someone that. Therefore, boyfriend will have to do.

Her brow creases as she slides off the console she's using for a seat and walks over with her sister in tow. "Are you sure it's for me? Roan didn't say anything about giving me a gift."

Shrugging, I step back so she can get to her gift. "Maybe he intended it to be a surprise." That makes sense, right? Surprises are fun and make people happy. Then again, I'm not sure if Draconian men understand the whole concept of a pleasant surprise. They're kind of regimented and plan everything out ahead of time with some detail.

Peering down into the box, Meiko begins shaking her

head. "I'd never feel comfortable wearing something like that and Roan knows it." Searching around inside, she looks for some indication of who sent it or who the intended recipient is. Coming up empty handed, she reaches for the communication unit attached to the shoulder of her uniform.

Roan's holographic image comes up. He appears to be sorting through foodstuffs somewhere. "Greetings, my queen. What do you wish of me?" His eyes wander over her body from head to toe, clearly admiring her tight-fitting albeit dirty uniform.

"The drones delivered a gift and we have no idea who it's from or which of us was supposed to get the gift."

He glances to the side, seeming annoyed. After a few awkward seconds he grabs his com device and begins scrolling through the handheld. "I will look through the list of deliveries and try to figure it out."

After a few moments he looks up. "All I see is a delivery was made into the hands of the intended recipient, Queen Daisy. It does not state her full title because the three of you have yet to select a name for this vessel."

Yeah, if we'd named the ship I would be called Queen Daisy of whatever the ship name is. Wait, did he say it was for me? Shocked, I step forward. "It was for me? Can you tell who sent it?"

Roan freezes in place. "I am uncertain, Queen Daisy. You have my apologies."

Meiko grins at me, nudging me with her arm. "Someone has a secret admirer. I wonder who it could be."

Roan looks from Meiko to me and back again, totally ignoring Aiko. I get the distinct feeling that I'm missing something but have no idea what it could be. "Well, that's really nice of someone. The dress is amazing and I really needed a pair of nice shoes. It feels weird to not know who sent them."

Roan sighs, "Perhaps it was a warrior who wishes to provide for a queen out of kindness. I do not believe you have shown interest in a male, so it is clear you need a temporary protector."

I look away, embarrassed. This is the Draconian version of charity. Unfortunately, I'm destitute. Accepting charity humbly is a sign of good character. My mother always said it was selfish not to allow others the privilege of giving.

"I really appreciate the gift and wish I could thank the gentleman in person. If anyone steps forward, please let me know."

"It will be as you command, Queen Daisy."

Shock and annoyance war for the top place in my emotions. "Hell's bells, I wasn't commanding or anything like that. It was more of a simple request."

Roan's smile turns indulgent. "You are nice and well worthy of a secret benefactor, Queen Daisy. If I learn the identity of your secret protector, I will encourage him to speak with you."

Meiko is still grinning from ear to ear. "Thanks, Roan. We're meeting for dinner, right?"

"Yes. That is my plan." His eyes flash to Aiko for the briefest of seconds before he continues. "It will be as you commanded with no little ones or sisters, just you and me on the human date." His expression can only be described as enthralled with my friend. The two of them are really adorable together. Aiko rolls her eyes and walks off grumbling.

Meanwhile, I lift the pretty dress from the box and hold it up to my body. Truth be told, it looks like it was custom-made for my form. My mind recalls us receiving a full body scan upon arrival. I'm totally awed that someone had the tailor bots make this specifically for me. Did they pick out the fabric and style or just type out a message and let the bots have at it?

Yeah, I'll admit to liking feminine things. I like soft fabric, pastel colors, and a few frills. This dress has just enough detail to make it sophisticated but not gaudy. Whoever thought I'd be rescued, much less gifted with something so beautiful? Holding the delicate fabric, the situation almost seems surreal.

Most of the women wear their pretty gowns when they're not working. My best guess is that after the hell they've been through, fixing themselves up is a way to put it all behind them and move forward in a more positive direction.

I honestly can't wait to wear mine. This is nicer than any piece of clothing I've ever owned. I feel guilty for coveting nice things when people back on Earth are having a hard time finding food. My rational mind kicks in, reminding me that I didn't buy it and there's no way I can transform this gown into food and get it to people on Earth, so I might just as well stop obsessing and enjoy it.

I try to imagine who might have given it to me. Maybe it's Cassandra, the woman in charge of everything around here. That's the kind of thing I would do if I were in charge. I'd make sure every single woman felt special and included. This idea makes real sense to me.

8 NEW OBSESSION

DARNOK

Roan shoots me an annoyed look before going back to making food boxes for the queens. "I do not know what you hope to accomplish by refusing to allow Queen Daisy to know you are her benefactor. Do you hope to confuse her into noticing you?"

I place another sweet confection into the box I'm building for my precious queen. Seeing her reaction to my gift made my chest ache with longing.

Carefully easing it from my huge scarred hand into the tiny space, my wings lift and tail freezes in place. I am pleased when it slides into place rather than breaking apart in my hand as several have done already. Grabbing another tiny bit of food, I continue filling all the empty spaces in the box.

Refusing to answer my longtime friend's question, I choose instead to complain. "Why is it that human queens prefer pretty food in bite-size pieces?"

Roan chirps out a laugh. "Draconian queens relish tearing apart food with their razor-sharp teeth and slicing it with their talons. Human queens have neither sharp teeth nor talons to aid them in eating. Their blunt little teeth couldn't tear off a piece of meat from the bone if they tried."

"I have noticed their lack of sharp teeth. Even their claws are delicate. They need us more than a Draconian queen ever did, both as protectors and providers. My Daisy would surely perish without a warrior to cover her."

"Then it is lucky for Queen Daisy that she has you."

My wings droop. "She does not have me though, does she? I am only watching over her temporarily until she selects a breeder."

"I have been meaning to talk to you about that. Have you not noticed that you are the only warrior she looks to? Surely that is not by accident."

"She is small and not of a size for one such as me. You have seen us stand side by side, so you well know what I speak of, Roan. I dare not hope for more than this moment in time. To serve as her unseen guardian is enough for me."

"My Meiko assures me that human women are accommodating of our oversized endowments."

"We are not oversized. Our endowments are proportionate to our overall size." Realizing that I am stating things he already knows, I switch the conversation to the task at hand. "Let us prepare food for our queens and not talk of such."

His quiet reply is what I have grown to expect from the gentle breeder. "When you are ready, come to me and I will share all the information I have gathered on human queens."

"Thank you, my friend." Dropping another treat into place, I ask curiously, "Do you think the queens will enjoy our meager offerings?"

Roan holds up one of the bits to view it in the light. "I was told this is similar to a human treat called bak-lava. It is made with the meat of a seed and sticky sweet fluid. My Meiko loves this tiny treat. I hope your queen will as well."

"If she does not, I will find something she does like." My mind is made up about caring for the tiny queen. "Queen Daisy needs to gain weight. I will fatten her up with many delicious treats. Then she will choose the best from among our males for her mate."

Though honest, that statement earns me another confused glance from Roan. Stopping to look into his face, I speak freely to my close friend. "It feels strange for me to be in a safe sector of space and able to focus on the simple pleasure of providing for a queen. Before there was so much danger in our lives from both our own queen and rival queens that I could barely relax enough to sleep at night."

"I know that feeling all too well, having been a breeder with young to protect. I am pleased that my hatchlings will know only the arms of a soft human queen. Now we have hope for a better future for ourselves and our scions."

"It feels like wallowing in luxury not to worry about death stalking my every move."

Our conversation is cut short when the door to the dining hall opens and my preferred queen enters with her two twin queen friends. Queen Daisy has the gown I sent her tucked under one arm, still in the box. She looks lovely even in the dark uniforms they insist upon wearing to perform work duties. I quickly finish the box I am making and set it aside, before backing away from the table. Meiko makes her way eagerly to Roan and squeals with delight to see the treat he has made for her.

My Daisy laughs effortlessly at the way she hangs on

him and allows Roan to feed her the tiny bits of food. I wish to feed my Daisy, but I know she will not want to look upon me, much less eat food from my scarred hand. A tiny part of my soul dies at that realization. Yet, I do not care as long as I can look upon her lovely form.

Her eyes search around and land on me. When her brows draw into a scowl, I turn and make my way to the door. Confident that Roan will ensure she gets her treat, I head for the loading bay to select another job. The evening is young and I am not yet ready to take to my sleeping platform.

My mind wanders over how I might best serve my queen. As I walk it occurs to me that she has no ornamentations to decorate her frail body. Draconian queens wear large ornate pieces of jewelry containing impressive gemstones. Naturally, a human queen would not be able to bear the weight of such large pieces of decoration, but she might enjoy something fitted to her size.

Branching off toward the bay that holds our treasures, I abandon the idea of selecting another work assignment in favor of seeking out materials to create something special for my new queen. Though I know she is not mine, for some reason I persist in thinking of her as mine in my own mind. Since no one can know my thoughts, I see no harm in my innocent little game.

One of our warriors is milling around, looking through crates. "Greetings, Direk. What has drawn you away from the helm this evening?"

Turning, his wings lift and his horns perk up. "I am seeking something warm for the queen I wish to notice me."

Moving forward, I help him lift the lid off a huge crate of trade goods. "I will help you locate something suitable."

We begin sifting through the multitude of supplies inside. I spy many items which might be useful for trade but few that would brighten a queen's day. "Which queen caught your eye, my friend?"

He stills, not responding and I know something is troubling him. Finally, he speaks in a low voice. "Her name is Tamera. She is alone with a small queen at her side. Though many warriors cater to her, I wish to distinguish myself from the rest."

"She has a hatchling?"

"Humans call them children, for they came not from the shell," he corrects me.

"Yes, of course. We must procure any items you feel will give her and the small queen comfort. Look at the bottom on the lutar. I see a piece of fur." We pull together and when it jerks free I see it is a snow-white fur from a huge beast. There is a small stack of them. I pull them all free and we spread them out, looking them over. "I do not know from whence these came, but they are soft and well cured. They would make a nice warm bed covering or even a cloak."

"My queen and her child are cold during the day as they move about the ship. I will take two of these to the clothing bots to have cloaks made for them."

"That is a sound plan. Although I had a mind to make her some decorative jewels, I may have a cloak made for Queen Daisy from the remaining fur as well."

Nodding his agreement with our plan, he jerks his chin toward the communications console. "Some of the males have begun collecting information from the queens about their customs and home world."

Excitement strums through my chest. "I wish to see this information to know best how to serve my queen."

We approach the console and begin reviewing the data. An image comes up of a strange creature that does not look quite real. Direk speaks before I can fully process what I am seeing.

"I believe this is a children's toy mean to simulate a real creature from their home world."

"It says bear, but it says children sleep with them." Rubbing my chin I can only think it is some type of primitive superstition meant to ward off the creature it represents. I'm strangely fascinated by this custom. We dig out small pieces of brown fur along with more white fur and head to the room that houses the bots tasked with creating textiles.

When we arrive, we approach the manufacturing bots and program the specifications we wish into the machine. They use the dimensions of each queen to create a properly fitting garment while we wait.

Direk and I ignore the whirl and clack of the bots as they work, focusing instead on this small semblance of a vicious animal from the human home world. The information in our database is fragmented because it's cobbled together from random bits of information gathered by our males. We confirm the furry creature is called a bear and the inside is stuffed with soft fibers. We learn that several of the females had bears with long floppy ears that they kept well into their adulthood.

Rubbing my chin, I scratch my back against the metal wall as think over whether Queen Daisy could benefit from such a gift. Since we are already in the manufacturing unit with enough fur on hand to create two such creatures, I decide to have the bots make one for my queen in case her bear was lost because of the abduction. I reason that if she does not care for my gift, she can give it to another or save it for her own child.

When the bots are finished with the cloaks, they are very different. Mine is formed in the shape of an actual cloak but Direk programed his to fit like a long jacket. Wishing I had thought of that, I fold the full-length cloak for my queen, noticing the bots added a soft lining to increase the wearer's comfort. I pay more attention when programming the specifications for the bear and select a larger and more impressive size to make up for the simplicity of the cloak.

Again, I find that my skills are lacking, for the navigator's creature is smaller but more finely made. Mine is larger than I anticipated and since the bots did not have quite enough brown fur, they substituted remnants of the white fur for the stomach hands and long floppy ears. To my eyes the creature looks strange. Direk's bear has dark glassy eyes but mine has large eyes made of impressive red gemstone. I realize rather quickly that if one does not specify every fine detail, the bots just select them at random with no eye to what is aesthetically pleasing.

Direk inspects my creature with a critical eye and I can tell he wishes to laugh. My wings flare out, letting him know that I do not appreciate his smug attitude. Thinking better of provoking my ire over such a trivial matter, he grabs his gifts and beats a hasty exit, leaving me standing there with my less-than-perfect first attempt hanging limply from my hand. Lifting it, I stare into its strange little face before tossing it aside.

Roan made programing the bots seem easy when he helped me create a gown for Queen Daisy. Stalking back over to the console, I program in requests for smaller creatures with random fabrics for skin and a wide variety of features. Several machines whirl to life all at the same time and they begin churning out strange creatures one after another. Each of them is the same uniform tiny size, about the size of my hand. I inspect each one before discarding it onto the ground where the bear sits leaning against the wall. Is it my imagination or is the strange creature smirking at me?

Before long I have a small selection of them piled on the floor. Voice-prompting the bots to stop production, I kneel and sort through them, wondering why I ever thought this was a good idea. My scarred hands seem all the more monstrous when holding one of these soft flawless gifts. After a while they all start to look alike to me. None jump out as particularly fitting for a queen. Grabbing a small hover box, I fill it with my creations.

An odd feeling of melancholy settles over me when I program a delivery bot to take them to Queen Daisy's quarters. Then I stop in my tracks, deciding instead to deliver them myself. A quick check of the ship's computer tells me she is in the map room looking at star systems with her friend queens and Roan.

I make my way carefully to her private suite and am shocked by how sparsely decorated it is. Getting on my com, I order extra everything for her room to be delivered immediately. Setting up an alarm on my com to alert me when she is near, I get to work cleaning and arranging her personal space. I'm vaguely aware that I might be infringing on her privacy, but I cannot accept her being in a space with no luxuries. It is not right for a queen to live this way.

When the drones arrive, I add thick padding to her sleeping platform, extra coverings and extra of the square soft things the queens covet. Some call them pillows and others refer to them as cushions. I load her platform with several and toss on a few of the creatures to keep her company. I add a small water reservoir beside the box of sweets I made for her. In her tiny compartment in the wall is the dress I gifted her with, as well as a small assortment of other items. Making a mental note to order more clothing for her, I drape her cloak across the end of her sleeping platform and slip out the door.

This entire day has been one long exercise in why warriors are not suitable to care for queens. Every single deed I perform is poorly done. Shuffling into my quarters, I pull off my clothing and step into my personal mister. As the cleansing unit fills with warm mist, I brace my hands against the wall and look down my long, scarred body. For the first time in my life, I wish that I was other than I am. Rubbing cleansing lotion over my bulky frame brings back memories, reminding me where each and every mark on my body came from. Why do I still ruminate over the pain of my early years?

Perhaps I should ask our healer if there is a way to force me to let go of the memories that haunt my mind. It is a weakness I cannot bear to face in myself. I'm fit only for fighting and friending. Still my cock rises at the prospect of mating. When I see Roan with his little spawn, I long for one of my own. A little son to share my space and teach the ways of battle would go a long way toward easing the pain in my heart.

Grasping my cock, I squeeze, jerk, and twist it in my hand. My head fills with images of Queen Daisy. Instead of shock and disgust in her eyes, there is acceptance and admiration. In my head, she spreads her long lovely legs and allows me to see what the gods have given her. My imagination fills the blanks in my head of what she looks like there. In the images in the database, human queens are fleshy and soft, their vent open and ready for what males most wish to put inside.

The images floating through my mind cause me to jet long ropes of seed against the misty walls as I rasp her name. Even in my addled state, I know my fantasy can never be. I am a monster and she is a queen. That is the reality of my life.

9 ADMIRER

DAISY

Walking around the huge room with a rounded ceiling, Roan shows us a huge star map they've gotten through a data link with a nearby world. It shows this entire region of space, including the location of Earth. I'm not keen on going back there, but I'm also afraid of what my future holds with the Draconians. I know that I should feel grateful for them rescuing us and I am, but a small dark part of my mind still thinks this is a trick. I fear they are only being nice to us until we find a planet and then the tables will turn. It's the reason why I've been relieved at not getting courting gifts. I don't want any of them to become fixated on me.

Gazing at the magnificent star chart twinkling above our heads, I realize exactly how vast our sector of space really is. Humans have gone from believing they are alone in the galaxy to meeting a half-dozen different life forms in the space of my lifetime. It's kind of awe-inspiring in a way, but terrifying nonetheless.

Seeing this huge Draconian male strutting around bare-chested in his long flowing pants makes me realize how different they really are. His large body is corded with muscles and they contract when he moves. God knows, the one who rescued us is even more bulky. Where Roan's body is streamlined in what I've always thought of as a swimmer's or runner's physique, Darnok is built like a world champion bodybuilder. They're both really tall. My head comes about to Darnok's lower chest.

Meiko is all eyes when Roan spreads his wings and flies up to point out something on the three-dimensional map. His wingspan is impressive, but all I can think about is Darnok's wings. His skin is muted purples and greens where Roan is more golden. Draconians come in all sizes and different blended colors. Their wings are really different as well. Some look like bat wings with translucent skin over some kind of skeleton. Others have a downy coating on their wings that I wouldn't exactly call fur or feathers, just a thicker, plusher skin. Roan has this, while Darnok's wings look more like bat wings. All the warriors have pliable horns that move slightly when they're emotional. I'm always careful of the large talons that sit on top of their wrists because they look lethal.

I can't help but wonder what my kindhearted rescuer is doing right now. Roan assured me that he recovered fully from his injuries already. I've not seen much of him. Every time I happen upon him, he's gone before I can get turned around to talk to him.

I'm not surprised that he's avoiding me, but I'd kind of like to talk to him every now and then. He's the only one besides Roan that I feel comfortable being around.

Aiko slides up beside me. "You look deep in thought. What are you thinking about?"

She's not someone I know well so I keep my response light. "Just thinking about how big the universe is. Even our small corner boggles my mind."

Glancing up, she appears a bit awestruck as well. "Seeing it all laid out this way really puts the distances between worlds into perspective." Pointing to Earth, she grins. "Look at it, way out in the middle of nowhere compared to the rest. How do you think that happened?"

I know she's referring to how similar we all are. "It seems like we're all bipedal, mostly breathe air, and speak with our mouths. We've mostly all got two arms and two legs and can even make babies together. That can't be a coincidence."

The gleam in her eye tells me she's as curious about this as I am. "The Draconians say their DNA was manipulated thousands of years ago and mixed with dragon DNA."

We both watch Roan lift Meiko into his arms and fly off with her. They circle the room a few times, laughing and talking together. "I have to admit that I can believe it's true."

Meiko nods. "Perhaps whoever manipulated their DNA manipulated everyone else's as well."

I have to admit she's right about that. "Whatever happened, it means we've got some choices when it comes to choosing a husband."

"You mean choosing between the Draconians and other species? I don't think it's a good idea to try to meet up with another species. The dragon guys are hot, healthy, and accommodating. That's enough for me."

"I don't disagree with that. I meant human women in general have their choice, not you and me in particular. If the Draconians turn out to be as nice as they seem, I don't have any qualms about selecting a hot dragon guy for a husband."

"Have you seen Roan's little ones?"

"No, I've not made it to the hatchery yet. I'm putting

that off because I don't want to get baby fever or anything like that."

Shooting her sister an irritated glance, Aiko mutters, "At least one of you has some good common sense."

I don't know what it is about her sister hooking up with Roan that's stuck in her craw, but Aiko's always got something negative to say about her sister's choice. Then again I've wondered more than once if we're trauma-bonded to the guys that saved our life. Meiko has not left Roan's side and I'm always thinking about Darnok. Maybe Aiko's concerns aren't that far off base.

When the two of them fall into a kissing fest, Aiko and I show ourselves to the door. The last thing lonely old me needs is to sit around and watch my friend hang all over her hot boyfriend. We separate ways shortly before I get to my quarters. I have a nice long stretch in front of my door before it slides open. I wonder if the system recognizes me when the door automatically opens or will it just open for anyone. I hope it's not the latter.

I stop short the moment my feet step over the threshold. Someone's been in my room and I ended up with a posh makeover. Walking into the room, my feet sink into a plush rug. Everything looks so nice. My eyes focus on my bed and I see something that looks like fur. It's a fur wrap of some sort and it's soft as a baby's bottom. Running my hands over the luxurious white fur, I think it's either real or the aliens are really advanced when it comes to simulating it. Lying back on the bed, I pull the fur over me and for possibly the first time, I'm truly warm.

Rolling over to get comfortable, I find myself staring into the face of an oddly appealing stuffed rabbit. Being on a spaceship full of aliens who seem to be working their asses off to integrate what they know about women with the tiny nuggets of information they wheedled out of us, I can't say I'm surprised to find that I've been gifted with such a creative and expressive gift. These dragon dudes are really trying to make us feel at home, and guilt eats away at me that I can't find it in my heart to truly trust them yet. I'm guessing that's because we spent months locked in a cage and were starved and beaten. That's the kind of abuse that stays with a person.

I run my fingers down the long white ears and realize it's the same fur as my wrap. Clearly these guys have never seen a bunny, because the ears are square at the end. Still, his red eyes ring true. I saw a rabbit once with black eyes that had a red cast to them. I cuddle the stuffed animal close to my chest and just enjoy the feeling of hugging it. I'm so warm and happy that I tumble off to sleep, still wearing my clothes.

I WAKE, in my warm cozy bed, feeling safe and secure. For once my sleep was not disturbed with nightmares of being caged, cold, and hungry. My tummy rumbles and I roll over and reach for the box of treats on my bedside table. I sit up and pull the fur around my body before tearing the lid off.

Being hungry brings back too many bad memories for me, so I toss several pieces of food in my mouth and chew furiously. Before being abducted from Earth, I ate like a lady, using a plate and flatware. There were only certain things I ate with my hands. Now, I'm totally off the chain in that regard. I'll eat with my fingers in a heartbeat and think nothing of it. Being changed bothers me because I worry that it makes me less than I was before.

Looking around at my new digs, I spy a tall clear

canister on my nightstand. It appears to contain water, so I grab it eagerly. Sure enough there is a little spout that pulls out, making it easy to drink without spilling. That's my clue that it's a drink and not fancy alien perfume or something along those lines.

Sucking a generous gulp into my mouth, I realize its hydration fluid, not water. The Draconians don't seem to have actual H_2O. They have something similar to what I remember as being an energy drink on Earth. It's not as potent but does have a slightly fruity taste. I don't mind one little bit after the fishy-tasting water I drank with the aquatics. All in all, I'm well satisfied with my lot aboard the Draconian vessel.

Looking around once more, I realize there are small stuffed animals sitting all around my room. They're scattered amongst my pillows, sitting on my bedside table, and tucked here and there. It's cute that whoever designed them took a little poetic license. Several are clearly alien animals and a couple appear to have been modeled after dragons. I should probably give a few of them to the children, but I honestly can't bear to part with any of them. Each one is unique and adorable in its own way. Heck, they probably got their own drone delivery of toys. They don't need mine. Does that make me a bad person? I'm treading the line there.

Putting away my food and drink, I head for the cleansing unit. I'm eager to wear my new dress just to see if I can tell by their reaction who gifted it to me. Roan already dropped a bug in my ear that it wasn't Cassandra. That's only leaves the Draconian males. I'm fairly certain that Cassandra is responsible for the room upgrade though. It was nicely done and whichever warrior she tasked with creating the stuffed animals did a fantastic job.

I love the mister. After being dirty for so long, I'm kind of fastidious about hygiene now days. After letting the unit run through a full cycle, it blows hot air to dry my body and hair. I run my fingers through it to make sure it gets as dry as possible.

Standing in front the shiniest wall in my quarters, I pull the new gown over my head and pull the magnetic fasteners closed. I like how it fits. It's less ball gown and more action hero in design. With splits that run up each side, the soft delicate fabric feels whisper-soft and allows me to move freely. It's just feminine enough without being froufrou. I slip on the matching shoes and roll up the matching fabric to cover my knees. Alien shoes are more like thigh boots, but they're really comfortable, so I don't complain.

On a whim I grab the cloak, toss it around my shoulders, and stroll out the door. The couple of bites I had to stave off the growling in my stomach have worn off and now I'm starved. I know the dining hall will be brimming with delicious food, so that's where I go.

Upon arriving, the first thing I notice is that my friends are nowhere to be seen. The second thing I notice is Darnok sitting at table in the corner with a warrior I don't recognize. I hurry to get a tray, hoping to sit with him.

10 APPROPRIATE DINING PARTNER

DARNOK

"I do not think we will have the opportunity to fight many glorious battles in this new sector of space." Valden is an older warrior who has not seen a battle in my lifetime. He has been tasked with protecting the hatchery when our ship is under fire. He's good at securing the hatchlings and keeping them calm. Still, his statement seems absurd to me.

Grunting, I shove a chunk of food into my mouth. "We've been victorious in battle since arriving in the Naxis. We saved a hundred and thirty human queens, who even now reward our warriors by choosing them for mating."

"In general, do not believe the beings of this sector see their queens as property. The aquatics that slipped into this sector from Exion space are the problem. Hopefully, the ones we defeated were the last of them." The older man seems keen on us not having to spend our lifetimes fighting.

"It does not matter where in the 'verse we are or if we defeated the last of the aquatics, queens will need protecting wherever we go." I keep my voice calm and respectful, though my chest aches at the thought of yet more delicate queens being in danger.

Suddenly, a tray thumps gently down on the table beside me. When I turn to greet the warrior joining us, I see it is a queen. Not just any queen, but the one I secretly provide for and protect. Queen Daisy is wearing the clothing I made for her and looks lovelier than I can ever remember seeing her. Before I can speak, Valden comes to his feet and backs away, murmuring his excuses. Naturally, I cannot leave as well, for it would be considered rude to leave a queen dining alone.

Keeping my head down, I continue eating. There is a good chance that my horrible scars will kill off her appetite. Therefore the less she is exposed to them the better. I slowly draw my wings back and my horns slip back tight against my head. Tucking my tail on the far side of my body seems like a good way to make myself appear smaller and less intimidating.

A soft feminine voice sounds off. "Are you still running from me?"

I freeze. Is that what she thinks? That I am somehow afraid of her? "I am not avoiding you, my queen."

Her amused voice responds gently, "Are you sure about that? It seems like every time I enter a room, you disappear."

Grappling with an explanation that is something approaching honest, I quickly explain. "I have no wish to offend."

"What in the heck does that mean?"

When I do not immediately answer, she seems to grift around for an answer herself. "You know we didn't go willingly with the aquatics, right?" My head slowly turns to look into her annoyed face. "We fought hard and got beat up more than once. It's not like we're stupid weak women who deserved what we got or anything."

Her words kill off a small piece of my soul. How could

she believe that we would think such of the human queens? I hastily allay her fears about such nonsense. "I never for a moment thought you did. No queen deserves to be harmed or held captive."

Her brow creases. "Then what are you afraid of saying that might offend me?"

Shaking my head, I couldn't pull my horns up right now if my life depended upon it. I hasten to explain myself to the beautiful queen. "I have no wish to offend you with my scars, especially when you are trying to eat."

The small piece of food in her hand tumbles back down to her tray. Her shocked eyes lock with mine. "What in the world are you talking about?"

"My appearance makes me an unfit dining partner."

Picking the bite of food back up, she shoots me a disapproving look. "You're not the first hot warrior I've dined with. You know that, right?"

I've been around the human females enough to know that hot means attractive. I also know from being around the others that what she says is not true. I am not acceptable as a male to them. They avoid looking at me or look quickly away, unable to mask their disgust. Perhaps she feels beholden to me for rescuing her. That sounds reasonable.

Another queen walks up to our table. She is wearing a long white fur overcoat and has a small spawn at her side that is similarly dressed. Ah, this must be the queen that Direk hoped to impress.

Shoving the last of my food into my mouth, I choke it down and come to my feet. It's clear I am annoying the very queen that I wish to care for and the only remedy is to withdraw. Now that a new dining partner has arrived, it is time to take my leave. I murmur, "Thank you for the nice words, my queen. If you will excuse me, I have work that needs doing."

She sighs, looking a bit forlorn. It's clear that my leaving makes her no happier than my staying. Queens confuse me. Pivoting on my foot, I force myself away from the three queens. There is a chute near the door where trays are reclaimed. Shoving my tray into the space, I slip out the door, unnoticed by most of the other diners. Daring one quick glance over my shoulder on the way out the door, I see Queen Daisy is watching me leave. Her expression is somehow warm and disappointed at the same time. Since that makes no rational sense, I decide that perhaps what I see is my own desire for her to warm to me, rather than what she actually feels.

Daisy

When Tamera sits down with her little one, I marvel that we are both wearing fur on a thus far furless spaceship. Maybe everyone got warm clothing and I am reading too much into my new gift.

Tamera tears a cute teddy bear from the little girl's clutches and sits it on the table for her look at while she eats. She pulls her little one's coat off and situates a small box of finger foods on the table in front of her, moving them around until they look nice and appetizing for her child. Turning to me, she dusts her fingers off before speaking. "What was that all about?"

I watch a few food crumbs fall from her fingertips into her food box. "What was what about?"

"Darnok runs for the freakin' hills every time you show up."

I push food around on my tray and shrug. "I don't think

he likes me very much." Thinking about it, I ponder out loud. "Maybe seeing me running around naked like a fool when he rescued us was off-putting. You know Draconian warriors don't really respect the weak."

She giggles, causing her daughter to look up at her and smile. "That's not what Direk says."

"Is Direk your new guy?"

She lifts her chin with a smug expression stamped on her lovely face. "He sure wants to be, but the verdict's still out about that."

Wrinkling my nose, I try to remember who he is. "I don't think I know which one Direk is?"

"I think of him as tall, dark, and handsome in my mind."

I snort a laugh. "That doesn't exactly distinguish him from the other warriors on this ship."

"They might all be tall and dark, but none are as good-looking as my Direk. He made us matching coats because I told him how chilled we get walking around the ship during the day."

"That was real sweet of him. I don't know why they don't just turn up the heat. This is a ridiculous problem to be having in such a high-tech environment."

"Direk says Draconian ships are designed to maintain the correct temperature to satisfy Draconian basal body temperatures, but they have adapted the life support to be within range for human anatomy as well. If it were any warmer bacteria might spread and become a health concern. He's smart and I guess it's just one of the compromises we're making for two species to coexist aboard this vessel."

I huff out an exasperated breath. "Oh really, is that what he says. Your new beau is a fountain of information. What else does he have to say about us coexisting?" I'm being way more snarky than I intended and I realize it the moment the words leave my lips. My shoulders droop and I shoot Tamera an apologetic look. Rather than being mad, she has a slightly devious smile on her pretty face.

"I'm glad you ask about what he's been saying. He mentioned you just last night."

I jerk to attention, worried that the warriors don't like me after all. "I hope it was nothing bad."

"It wasn't anything bad." Glancing down, she shoves the toy back to keep her little one from grabbing it with sticky hands. "He told me all about how he met up with another warrior and they dug up these furs from the trade stock in one of the storage bays. They found it totally by accident and had our coats made by some manufacturing bots."

I freeze in place with a bite of food halfway to my mouth, shocked that she knows the information I most want to have. She knows the identity of my gifter.

Her expression turns smug. "I heard you got a big ugly bear, kind of like the warrior who made it for you."

At first I'm thoroughly confused and then the anger sets in. The thought of judging the warriors on their looks really rubs me the wrong way. "I wouldn't say any of them are particularly ugly and I happen to think the bear they made for me was really adorable. Sure he's made from two different kinds of fur and his ears are square, but other than that he's real nice."

She simply stares at me without blinking.

Lifting my chin slightly, I inform her with quiet dignity, "My bear has character and I like him."

"You should, sugar. That scarred-up warrior you're always asking about made both the bear and that wrap you're wearing. Word on the street is he's not very competent at programming the bots. I guess that's why you ended up with a cloak instead of a coat."

Anger boils in my gut. "He did just fine. I like the cloak better because I can use it for an extra blanket at night. That bear he made is big enough to use as a pillow." Reaching over to take a sip of my hydration packet, I clear my throat. "Last night was the best night of sleep I've had in years."

"Well, unless you want to end up mated to that monstrosity, you best stop accepting jacked-up gifts from him. You know how these guys are; if you accept their gifts they think you like them."

I'm so angry that I don't trust myself to speak. When she turns to help her child again, I grab my tray, fast walk to the strange recycling hole in the wall, and angrily shove it in.

Why does every blasted person on this ship think Darnok is some kind of big brawny monster? I've got eyes and I see how they all treat him, like he's an eyesore or some kind of alien killing machine.

We have rent your enemies limb from limb. His growly words circle around in my head, coming back to haunt me just when I need them least. Okay, so maybe he is a stone-cold killer, but he fought for our freedom. God knows those aquatics weren't going to let us go of their own accord. I can't stop thinking about it and don't really know what to do with myself. Since I'm not appropriate company and too upset to stay on task, I head back to my tiny space. Being alone sounds really good about now.

As I approach the door to my quarters I see none other than Darnok himself. He reaches out one hand as if to trip the door release but seems to think better of it. Instead he places something on the floor in front of my door. Squatting there at my door with his wings raised up, he looks every inch the dark angel come to rescue me again. His hand darts out to grab the item he laid down. He moves it to the side and leans it against the wall. I realize he's worried I'll stumble over it when I leave my room. Only, I'm not in my room.

Rushing forward, I call out his name. "Darnok, please wait, I want to talk to you."

He comes gracefully to his feet with the item in his hand. His eyes dart around for a second before he speaks. "Greetings, Queen Daisy."

I'm excited and breathless by the time I get to him. "Greetings, Darnok, it's good to see you again. What do you have there?"

Looking down at the handheld tablet in his hand, it takes him a minute to gather his thoughts. "It is a data pad that I loaded with information on Draconian culture and customs. There's a schematic of the ship and I marked the way to the bridge and room where the star charts are kept." He sneaks a glance at me and lowers his eyes again. "I thought it might ease your way."

Reaching out, I grasp the end closest to me. It takes him a second to let it go. God, we're all kinds of awkward together. "I'd like to talk to you for a minute if you have time."

"I believe three human minutes are the equivalent of a Draconian micron."

I grin at him, because he's kind of adorable when he babbles. "Yep, that's what my translator's telling me."

"My apologies, Queen Daisy. I did not mean to be redundant." Instead of an expression of remorse, he's looking kind of turned on. My belly does a little flip of excitement when his eyes crawl hungrily over my body. I'm sure he doesn't realize he's doing that.

Holding the data pad to my chest, I ask, "Will you come in and speak with me?"

Taking a step back, he murmurs, "I shouldn't."

"Please."

His eyes close, but he nods and follows me into my personal space. Though I'm usually slightly cold, right now the room seems too hot. I pull off the cloak and drape it over the foot of my bed. The only other furniture in the room is a small settee and square table and two chairs off to the side. Darnok is still hovering at the door. I get the feeling that if I chastised him for something, he run out the door and be halfway across the ship before I could stop him. Why the hell he's so panicky is anyone's guess.

I gesture to one of the chairs and he stalks over quickly and sits. His powerful legs eat up the distance in three steps. I gather a couple of hydration packets and my box of sweets —the sweets I now suspect he made for me—and sit on the opposite side of the table.

He's a bit jumpy. "How may I serve you, Queen Daisy?" His voice is deep and raspy. God help me, it makes my girly bits stand at attention. Absolutely filthy images float through my mind. Chewing my bottom lip, I ponder all the ways I can let him serve.

11 THE HUMAN KESS

DARNOK

Forcing my face into a neutral expression, I will my mouth to not say stupid things. I had to force myself not to kneel before her in the corridor. Queen Cassandra has made it clear that warriors are not to bow and humble themselves before a queen. We were schooled that human females find overt displays of submission distasteful. My natural instinct was to drop to my knees and offer her my service. I suspect that my reward for controlling myself was being invited into her personal space to speak with her. I never thought to be alone with a queen, much less the queen of my dreams.

My brethren would never believe that all it takes to make a battle-hardened warrior quake in his boots is a sweet human queen staring him in the eyes. Her expression is soft and pensive, as if she is deciding to do or not do something important. Whatever it is she wants, I have already decided that I will comply with her request. Whether she wishes riches, a more spacious room, or even her own ship, I will see she gets it.

Finally, she speaks. "I wanted to thank you for the data

pad, clothing, all the nice stuffed animals, and all the other nice things you did for me."

"I live to serve, my queen."

Baring her blunted teeth to me, she continues. "You saved me from a fate worse than death, killed all of those asshole aquatics that tormented me for so long, and now you're looking out for me aboard this ship. I appreciate that more than you can possibly know."

Something loosens in my chest, enabling me to breathe easier. "It is my pleasure to serve you until you chose breeders."

The corners of her mouth turn down. "I hate that word."

My brain scrambles to correct my offense. "I mean to say that it is my pleasure to support you in any way you wish until you chose breeders." I smile, careful to conceal my sharp teeth. Although she did make the mating gesture to me by showing all her teeth, I do not believe she knows what she does.

When she laughs, the sound is like beautiful music to my ears.

"I can't believe you thought 'serve' was the word I hated." Shaking her head, she states with a wave of her hand, "It's the word 'breeder' that I can't stand."

"You hate breeders?" I honestly can't keep the shock from my expression or voice. What kind of queen dislikes breeders? It makes no sense to me. "Breeders are kind-hearted and clever males. They are bred to see to the care and feeding of a queen." I stop talking because she is frowning at me.

"I like them as people. It's just the word that I don't like."

"Though you explain, I am more confused than ever."

"The word breeder implies that it's their primary job or something."

She does not understand, so I clarify. "Breeding for their queen *is* their primary responsibility."

"It seems disrespectful."

I don't know what to say that will not seem as though I'm arguing with her, so I remain silent.

She leans over the table slightly. Her expression is happy and carefree. "This is the point where you're supposed to ask if I like warriors better."

Shocked, I do as she suggests. "Do you prefer warriors to breeders?" It seems like such an absurd question that I wonder if she is testing me.

Sitting all the way back in her seat, she nods. "I like one warrior in particular."

The perversion of queens never ceases to amaze me. Many of the human queens have passed over breeders in favor of warriors, even Queen Cassandra. Therefore, I do not know why I'm surprised that Queen Daisy prefers warriors as well. "I am certain he will serve you well, my queen."

"I'm not so sure about that. He's really standoffish and runs away every time I enter the room. Any suggestions on how I can get him interested in spending a little time with me?"

Something sick curls in my gut, for I think that she is speaking of me. I am certainly the only warrior running from a queen on this ship. My mouth goes dry, but I stammer the most helpful reply I can think of in the spur of the moment. "Perhaps you should just tell him bluntly of your decision. He will fall into line." My wings drop and I am in wonder at myself for suggesting such. Surely she means someone other than me.

Rather than responding to my suggestion, she glances around the room. "I really like all the stuffed animals you made. Do you mind if I ask why you made so many of them?"

"I kept hoping the abominations we call bots would manufacture an aesthetically pleasing one."

She chuckles again. It's such a nice sound. "I think they're all unique and have character. Do you know what that means?"

"You do not like things that are too similar in appearance?"

"You got it, handsome. That's one of the reasons why I like you."

Though initially stunned, I recover quickly. "It is logical that you are mistaking gratitude for fondness. I saved you from the aquatics, but you do not owe me attention."

"You're not listening and that makes me sad."

I jolt forward. "It is not my intention ..."

"I really like you." She stares at me as if waiting for me to catch the meaning of her words.

I glance away, stating quietly, "I like you as well, Queen Daisy."

"You can call me Daisy."

I am prepared for this request because all the queens make it from time to time. "Yes, my queen."

"I honestly like you, Darnok." She acts as though repeating the statement will drive home some point I can't quite fathom. Bewildered, I try to imagine where this conversation is going.

She stands, walks around the table, and brings her hand up to my chin. Tilting my head back to look into her eyes, she glances down at my lips. Images of the human *kess* jump forward in my mind. I have seen Queen Cassandra make the human kess with her takadon. Mathadar seems quite taken with her ways. Queen Daisy standing over me looking at my lips makes me forget for a brief moment that I am hideous.

My lips are not scarred and she clearly likes them. My tongue comes out to swipe slowly over my bottom lip. Her eyes jump to mine and then drop back down to watch my tongue moving over my lip. She's somehow caught in my thrall and I don't know how I accomplished that exactly. It seems as though I am teasing my lovely queen and luring her into making the kess with me. I like how powerful having this bit of control over her makes me feel. According to the teachings of my people, that makes me a very bad male.

Her head drifts down and she stops just before making contact with my lips. "I more than like you." Her lips move over mine and I know a kind of pleasure I never once dreamt of before. Her mouth is warm and hungry for me. She nibbles at my bottom lip with her blunted teeth.

Is this the message I sent by licking my bottom lip earlier? If it is I shall do nothing else when we are together. She uses her tongue to coax me into opening my mouth and then explores my mouth in ways that make my cock hard.

My tail trails up her leg and around her waist, pulling her into my lap. It's a bold move but I'm only dimly aware of what I am doing at this point. My queen comes easily into the circle of my arms and sits on my legs. She weighs practically nothing and I like having her close. We make the human kess for I know not how long before she pulls back. Her lips are pinker and swollen from all my bold kesses. She has a happy dreamy look in her eyes that makes me think I should talk less and kess more.

"Are you well, my queen?"

Her lips turn up into a small but satisfied smile. "Me? I'm better than I've ever been in my entire life."

I can't keep the smile off my face. She likes being in my arms. Others will not believe that and if I weren't here I'd not believe it either.

"How about you? How are you holding up?"

That wipes the smile immediately from my face. "I am well, but you should not share such intimacies with me. You need a…"

"Don't say it." A small pout contorts her face into an adorable expression. "I know you must like me because you take care of me and kissed me back. I'm interested in you, so don't tell me to find myself another male without taking a little time to get to know me. It hurts to be dismissed out of hand."

Pulling her closer, I tuck her head under my chin. "I have no wish to hurt your emotions, my queen."

"Then you'll stay?"

My hands clasp around her, digging slightly into her skin. She wishes me to stay and delve into perversions I've not dreamed were possible with a queen. All my self-loathing and doubts evaporate in the face of this new opportunity to know intimacy with a queen. "I wish to stay at your side for as long as you will have me, my queen."

She relaxes into my arms and I decide to seek out more comfortable seating for us. Standing, I walk across the room and sit on the settee with her still in my lap. "You feel good in my arms."

"That's good because I like being close to you. What would you like to talk about?"

"I wish to make more of the human kess with you." No sooner are the words out of my mouth than I realize how forward I'm being.

Looking momentarily confused, an expression of understanding quickly jumps onto her face. "You want to keep kissing? I'm down for that. How about we each share interesting facts about ourselves and kiss in between?"

"I do not believe I would be able to enjoy many kesses if we do such, for I have very few interesting things to share about myself."

"That can't be true. Let me start. Did you know I was assigned to work with the military on Earth?"

"I can't imagine you as a warrior. You are often timid."

A haunted expression passes over her face. "I'm afraid the aquatics beat all the bravery right outta me."

"If I could kill them all again, I would for daring to harm you."

Her facial expression brightens. "That's a sweet thing to say. I know you say things like that because you were raised to think like a warrior."

"Did you never kill anyone when you were in uniform?"

She shakes her head. "I actually worked for the Northern United Provinces government. They assigned me to work with a military detachment because they needed a linguist. I speak five Earth languages. We were considered adjunct staff, not warriors. I barely got any training in hand-to-hand combat and weapons. It was more like going through the motions, so I would understand the procedures they used."

"I see. You had a special skill, so the other warriors protected you during the battles." I'm pleased that she is looking at my lips again.

Her eyes rise to meet my own and I see true admiration in her pale blue eyes. "It's kissing time again," she announces eagerly.

I do not need to be encouraged in this pleasurable

endeavor. Leaning down, I meet her lips halfway. She climbs face-first into my lap and I can barely contain my excitement. This time when she makes the human kess with me, she runs her hands up and touches my horns. If I thought my cock was hard before, it is nothing compared to the painful stiffness she is perched upon now.

Her hand drifts down to squeeze me there, as if to test that I am ready for breeding. She murmurs, "You do come prepared, don't you?"

Though I do not know what this means, I eagerly agree. "My cock is always prepared to pleasure you, my sweet queen."

She pulls back long before I have had my fill. "Now it's your turn to tell me something about yourself."

I am stunned because I thought perhaps she was joking about wishing to know about my life. I say the first thing that comes to mind. "Our former queen dug her claws into me for the pleasure of seeing if I would scream." Lifting my chin, I state proudly, "I did not."

Before I can decide if she is proud of that accomplishment, she is making the human kess with me again. This time there is a depth of emotion that was not there before and a hint of desperation in her movements. It dawns on me that she is emotionally harmed by the knowledge I imparted. I hold her close and part my lips from hers. Our foreheads touch as I try to console her. "I am well now, my queen. Instead of a vicious Draconian queen, I now have sweet queen who gives kesses instead of pain."

"You didn't deserve to be hurt. You know that, right?"

"I do know that and came to terms with what happened long ago. Do not let it drain the joy from this moment, my precious. It is in the past." Trying to distract her, I remind her of our kessing game. "It's your turn to share an interesting fact about yourself."

"I almost got killed by a crocodile as a child. During summer vacation, I was walking by a river and not paying attention. A huge one ran up and would have had a bite of me if it weren't for my father."

"What is this creature you speak of?"

"They live near the water and eat meat. Crocs will grab you in their huge jaws and roll you under the water over and over again until you drown. When you're dead, they drag you back onto land and eat you."

"I do not like these creatures." Clutching her close, I have lost the will to kess with her. Thinking of her being dragged under the water in the manner she describes stays with me for a bit. In an effort to put it out of my mind, I share information about myself again.

"I never set foot on a planet until I began going on trade missions as an adult warrior. Most Draconian males are born on the ships and live their whole life traveling around the space surrounding our home world. It is one reason I am so eager for Queen Cassandra to locate a planet for us to call home. We must be careful to thoroughly investigate all the animals. I will not have dangerous beasts trying to kill my queen."

"Queen Cassandra has her own male to look out for her. You don't need to worry about her." I sense the disapproval in her voice. Dare I hope that she is jealous?

Putting my fingers under her chin much like she did to me earlier, I tilt her head back. "I was referring to you, my lovely queen."

Her eyes turn warm and approving again. It makes me think that perhaps I am not so inept at pleasing a queen after all.

This little queen seems to like being in my arms well enough, and I certainly enjoy having her there. I succumb to the overpowering urge to kess with her again. This time when our lips join, it is slow and sensual. Each time we kess it is subtly different. I cannot decide which I prefer. Her delicate scent becomes stronger and muskier, provoking my own mating scent to rise.

Perverse ideas float through my mind and images of me making the human kess with the tender flesh between her legs is foremost among them. The scent coming from her sex is mouthwatering, making me desperate to taste her on my tongue.

Unbidden, my tail slides up her bare leg and I discover some type of thin fabric covering the area I most want to touch. She opens her legs to give me better access and makes an alluring needy sound against my mouth. Knowledge flashes through my mind that she needs me to pleasure her. Wrapping my wings around her to lift her slightly, my hands find their way up her long gown, shoving it up around her waist. The bulbous tip of my tail has already looped around the side of the soft fabric and is pulling it down her thighs. I feel her lips on my neck and her hands pulling apart my uniform top. Shrugging out of it with her help, I let it fall to my waist. Not wishing her to focus on my scars, I tilt her face up and take her lips again.

Her eager hands delve into the front of my uniform and she strokes my thick cock with both hands. My fingers are already slicking through her tender folds. She's wet for me. I don't know why I'm surprised by that. Unable to resist, I pull out one hand and bring my fingers to my mouth. Pulling back slightly, I taste her at long last. Her flavor bursts over my tongue even as her breathless voice sounds off in my ear.

"I can't believe you just did that."

Sucking greedily once more, I push my thick cock into her hands harder before making an aggressive human kess with her again. I murmur between kesses, "Taste yourself on me." When I shove my tongue into her mouth, she sucks at it, making that tiny needy sound again.

I force her back and immediately move down her body, tugging my cock free of her grasp. The beautiful gown I made for her covers everything a warrior would wish to see, but her queenly bits are calling to me. I revel in the scent for a moment before turning to kess one silken thigh. She laughs, telling me she's ticklish there.

Sighing, I target her lush folds with my tongue, licking leisurely down the glistening seam of her sex. Her delicate hands come down to part herself for my inspection, her finger pointing to a tiny nub hidden within. It feels like she's telegraphing her desires straight into my mind. Leaning back down I lavish the round nub with attention by licking, sucking, and eventually running one coarse finger over it lightly.

She jerks roughly in my arms, moaning my name. I consider it verification that she likes my gentle ministrations. Her hands drift down to my horns and I know a kind of pleasure I never dreamed of before this moment. I'm far too interested in tasting her to stop. This is everything a warrior could ever desire, resting right here on my tongue. Sweeping down, I discover all her sweet spots before sucking on the nubs that clearly brings her the most pleasure once more.

Her legs tremble and the moment I penetrate her with a thick scarred finger, her legs lock around me and she seizes up in a strong climax. When she screams my name, pure male pride surges through my chest at having pleased a queen so well. I'm intent on cleaning away all her tasty juices with my tongue when she relaxes. This is happiest and most peaceful I've ever felt in my entire life. Some warriors believe in a hereafter where the queens adore us as much as we adore them. I never dared to believe that was possible before this moment. Now I think we have found such in the here and now with our human queens.

Suddenly klaxons sound off, loud and harsh in our ears. Flashing emergency lights pull me from my philosophical musings and my queen from the dreamlike stupor of being pleasured by me. Thinking only of protecting this newfound love, I roll to my feet and head for the door.

"Where are you going?"

Glancing over my shoulder, I explain quickly. "Our ship is under attack. I must lock you inside, my queen. Stay safely ensconced in this room and I will return for you when the emergency is over."

Locking the door securely behind me, I rush to the central hub knowing full well that locking up a queen is forbidden. My head is filled only with thoughts of protecting my new queen and her queen friends. Nothing else matters to me.

12 NOT STAYING PUT

DAISY

Whatever's going on, Queen Cassandra will network with Meiko and Aiko to coordinate a battle strategy. Shame fills my chest as I realize that I'm the only one not jumping into the battle. The cold hard fact is, I've got no fight left in me. I'd be more of a distraction or the weak link in the chain if I went to the bridge. Also, two women on the bridge is a bit of a crowd, but three is a disaster in the making. We'd be tripping over each other and the warriors wouldn't know who to listen to. The twins are highly motivated and seem to enjoy a good fight.

I grudgingly admit that we're all better off with me leaving them to it. Still, I feel a little useless sitting around wringing my hands in my lap like a helpless victim when there's danger about.

Though Darnok made it abundantly clear that I'm not supposed to go out of the room, doing absolutely nothing during an emergency seems imprudent. Surely there is something I can do to help when the ship's being attacked. After pacing around for a bit, I decide to sneak down to the hatchery. The males will be running a skeleton crew and likely in need of an extra set of hands.

I unlock the door easily, since the system is set for females to override every command that a male codes into it. They think just because we're women, we're trustworthy. I'm not sure that's true. I head out into the hallway and it's a freaking ghost town. Swallowing thickly, I realize whatever the emergency is, it's taking every available warrior to handle. Up until now, they've never left us alone, particularly when there is any level of danger. I make my way across the ship, wondering about what kind of threat would be significant enough to draw every abled-bodied male to the front lines of this battle.

I jump onto a lift and drop down two floors to the hatchery. When the lift aligns with the floor, I see through the glass that total chaos is reigning on that entire floor. When the door opens, I rush into the main room. Valden steps out to meet me. "You have come to help with the little ones, have you not?"

"Yeah, what the heck is going on?"

"We are under attack by an unknown enemy vessel. Queen Cassandra believes that having so many queens on board is drawing the notice of every pirate and unsavory character in the area."

I can see the hatchery and yell to be heard over the chaos. "What can I do to help?"

There is silence for a brief second as he snags a really young hatchling from the air and tucks the little one under one arm. He squeals and flails his wings, trying to escape. I reach out and pluck the babe from his grasp and hold his tiny face up to mine. He goes perfectly still and I realize it's because I'm a queen in his little eyes. Was he taught to fear females? It seems so, because he's frozen in place.

Valden is going on and on about how Draconian young mature on a faster timeline than human children, and because of that their hormone levels are extremely high. It apparently makes it difficult for them to calm down during times of stress. He's talking about how they're gonna put them in a circle and teach them a new song.

Suddenly the little one decides I'm no threat. I know this because he leans out and licks the tip of my nose. A laugh bubbles up and bursts forth before I can stop myself. This seems to intrigue the little one even more. It's cute at how focused he is on me. An idea pops into my head. "Are the hatchlings sensitive to noise?"

The older man waves one hand through the air. "Obviously not, Queen Daisy."

"I mean are they sensitive to high-pitched noises?"

He shakes his head, clearly exasperated.

Bringing two fingers to my mouth, I let loose with the loudest and longest whistle that my lungs can support. The room grows quiet as the last few rambunctious hatchlings turn to gape at me. Looking around the room, I can see several dozen small Draconian children, all male, have quieted somewhat. They're all so different. Some have wings so small that it seems improbable they could support their bodies in flight. The little one in my arms makes a squeaking noise and I cuddle him close to my chest. He nuzzles his tiny face against my neck and stretches his legs down like an exhausted puppy. This one's all tummy and scrawny limbs with his wings fluttering slightly behind him.

I quickly try to think of what might distract them besides me, because I get the feeling seeing a queen up close is already wearing thin for them. "Everybody come sit in the center of the room. It's time for an ancient Earth custom called story time."

One of the older kids steps forward. He might be around nine or ten and he reminds me of Roan with his golden skin. "My sire has mentioned you, Queen Daisy. The Draconians have tales of our ancient kin as well."

I head for the center of the huge room, speaking over my shoulder. "Oh, these aren't stories about real people. Earth stories are created from our imagination and they're all fantastical adventures."

The know-it-all tone in his voice is replaced with one of interest. "Young warriors love action and adventure."

Most of the spawn begin following us and the adult males begin wrangling the rest of them. A few of the really small ones fly over and around me, their tiny nostrils flaring. They're trying to figure out what I am. It drives home that few of the women have visited the hatchery. I reach out my hand to one and he lowers himself into my palm. I cuddle him against my side with one arm and sit down cross-legged. Several more land and come crawling into my lap. Most of the others sit on bended knees, whispering to one another. I can tell they're still antsy because their little wings and tails never stop moving.

Halfway into my story about a horrible beast who keeps a beautiful human woman locked in his castle with only talking furnishings to keep her company, the emergency lights inside our room start blinking. The males immediately begin gathering up the smallest of the hatchlings. The older children begin to help and almost before I can get to my feet, they are opening the entire back wall. Several panels slide open to reveal half a dozen tiny safe rooms. I can tell that's what they are because the walls are armored like the shuttles they fly around in. There are also some incubators built into the back wall, and large square metal emergency boxes mounted on the walls.

Valden motions me over. "These are emergency pods. They are designed to release if and when the battle is lost or the doors to the hatchery are breached."

I begin helping them squirrel away small groups of the little ones, each with a male caretaker. "I guess that means they're about to blow."

Shoving an older boy into the first pod, he nods. "We must act quickly, before the doors are breached. I will stay to secure the last pod."

"Jesus, you mean someone has to stay behind? That's a seriously shitty design flaw."

"It was designed by queens who did not value the males who cared for their young. We were expected to see her breeders and young to safety and then join the battle."

Helping him ease several more children into another pod and seal it, I can see it all in my mind's eye. This old man is going to die trying to save us. His strong hand comes out to gently pull one of the newborns from his little habitat and Valden carefully hands him over to another caretaker. Before letting the little one go completely, his hand brushes over the babe's head, almost like a silent blessing. Valden's wings are tight against his back, his horns are standing straight up, and the expression on his face is one of pure love and devotion. He wears his heart on his sleeve. I swallow thickly to witness such vulnerability.

Though I'm quickly becoming an emotional wreck, the old man seems little bothered by the fact that he'll soon be dead. The unfairness of this situation breaks my heart into a thousand painful pieces. I can't believe this is happening. Out of nowhere my fight comes roaring back.

I get busy, helping close the pods. We have only one remaining when I get shoved roughly into it by Valden. Now it's down to just me and a tray containing three large eggs. I hold out my arms, intent on doing what I can to save them. Valden gestures to something behind me. "Place each in an incubator and trigger the automatic settings." He hesitates and I can see how he feels about entrusting the eggs to a female. It takes every ounce of self-control the old man has to reach for the button that activates the locking mechanism.

I whisper emotionally, "Don't worry. I'll protect them with my life."

No sooner do I speak the words than the door bursts open and someone shoots the locking mechanism with a laser rifle. Valden steps between me and our attackers. With a quick movement of his wrist, a laser pistol appears. I can't see what's going on, but I know it's going to be bad.

Hoping to protect the eggs, I rush to the back of the unit and begin opening the incubation units. My hands are trembling. The sound of fighting rings in my ears and suddenly a huge shadow looms over me. Leaning over to protect the eggs, I realize my small body is not enough. A quick glance over my shoulder reveals nothing but the shadow. Letting out a shaky breath, I think that maybe I'm letting my imagination run away with me. There's no such thing as shadow people, right?

It's then that an invisible hand closes around my arm and it becomes clear the person is using some kind of technology that renders him invisible to the human eye. He jerks me away and I allow it, hoping whoever it is won't notice or be interested in the eggs. Each of the three contains an unborn Draconian, one female and two males.

My hopes are dashed when he pulls me out and I see more shadows moving around. One is standing over Valden's prone body, and another appears to have removed the eggs from the tiny incubators built into the back of the escape pod. He is transporting the eggs.

Panic sets in because I can't let them get away with taking those hatchlings. Turning my body, I lash out with every ounce of energy I can muster. I hit, kick, and scratch, all the while screaming the walls down. All that expended effort only earns me a smack upside the head from my assailant. It's enough to leave my ears ringing, my vision blurred, and my legs struggling to keep me upright.

Now is the moment I usually just give up, but something new fires to life in my gut again. I remember how Meiko kept fighting and never gave up. If she can do it, there's no reason in the world I can't do the same. They might win, but I'll make them bleed for taking those babies.

I grab some kind of mechanical device from a shelf as we go past. Pointing the device straight ahead, I begin pushing buttons. A healing beam begins scanning the person in front of me. Damn, it's just my luck to end up with a healing unit when I need a laser scalpel or something equally lethal.

My new abductor slaps the medical device from my hand, making a guttural sound that I interpret as irritation. Well, screw him. I'm sick and tired of playing the part of a good little victim. I lunge forward. The moment our bodies collide, I realize what a colossal mistake it was to try and take him down that way. He's stout and rock-hard.

A hand comes out hard and fast around my throat. I kick toward where I think his groin might be. He growls a warning in some language that's not been programmed into my translator and begins to squeeze. Then again he may be speaking an obscenity that isn't programmed into the system. This is the moment I've dreaded, the one where I have to decide for myself what I'm made of. Do I continue to fight a battle I'm destined to lose, or submit?

My body makes the decision for me. My nails claw from his hand backward, drawing blood. My feet begin climbing up the front of his body even though I can't see him. I kick at what I hope is his face. My fingers slip in the blood I'm drawing from his hands. Ha, you'd think the idiots would use armored gloves or something. The hand releases, roughly shoving me away.

I lose my balance and land on my ass with a self-satisfied smirk on my face. Then I remember why I'm fighting so hard. Rolling to my feet, I go for the shadow carrying the eggs. The tray has no protective covering, so I know a full-frontal assault might result in damaging them.

Turns out, it doesn't matter. A moment after hearing a loud thud, the back of my head explodes with pain. The lights go dim and I'm vaguely aware of being slung over someone's shoulder. My hip scrapes on something rough and I can't lift my hands to fight anymore. My mind drifts and I imagine myself on my feet and fighting again. At this point, all I care about is getting those eggs back and getting as far away from these nameless, faceless bastards as possible.

My foot collides with the hard metal floor, jolting me awake. Shoving myself off the floor with two hands, I get to my feet. I don't know what happened while I was out, but it looks like Valden came to and followed us. He's sprawled on the floor again, with one hand reaching toward a strange alien shuttle. My heart seizes in my chest because I can tell he's dead this time. The old man looks frail in a way he didn't when he was alive and his skin has a pale sick pallor to it. Tears spring to my eyes and I try to get to him. Maybe if I do chest compressions or something, I can get him back.

Putting one foot in front of the other, I fling myself forward only to be snatched up by a shadowed alien twice my size. He's got me tucked under his arm like a rag doll. I reach out for Valden, even though he's dead and I have no hope of getting to him.

We board the shuttle and I can feel it lifting off even before I get dumped into a seat. Tears burn my eyes but I force myself to think. *God, Daisy, you're not stupid*, I chide myself. I need to figure a way out of the situation.

It's clear that I need to change up tactics. If I keep fighting, they'll keep knocking me out. If I bide my time and study the enemy, I might be able to brainstorm a way out of this awful mess. Since I'm no longer on the Draconian ship or under the protection of Darnok, I'll have to save myself and those little ones. My eyes begin searching for the little ones still growing in their shell. The poor babes are totally unaware of the danger they're in.

13 ESTRANGEMENT

DARNOK

Sliding to a stop inside the bay doors, my eyes search for the slight human queen who captured my heart. The space behind me fills with warriors and as I gape at the carnage before me, they spill around me rushing to help the dying and see to the dead. There are over twenty strong warriors scattered about and my chest constricts to know that even with all the blood spilled this day they were not able to save the human queen or our young.

Pharon kneels and pain lances through my chest when I see him pull out a funeral stasis unit. The small elongated pods are color coded to differentiate the living from the dead when they are immobilized in a stasis field.

My feet are moving before my mind wills it so, and I'm forced to push past the throng of warriors to get to him. Crossing the cavernous bay seems to take forever, and then suddenly I am looking down at Valden's body. My wings draw up painfully behind my back when I realize that he gave his life trying to protect the young ones he loved so much. Squatting down, as the dark smoky stasis field envelops him, it dawns on me that he was also trying to protect my queen. It is a life debt that I will gladly repay.

Swallowing down my pain, I come to my feet with renewed purpose. Direk appears at my side with a scanner in his hand, giving a report. "We have the ship back. No alien bodies were recovered, and the death count stands at seventeen with forty-three wounded, sir."

"What of the alien ship?"

"They are gone, sir, along with your queen."

"She cannot be gone." Images of her writhing beneath me rise in my mind, her legs parted and welcoming. Shaking my head once, I snarl. "I do not accept that."

Direk's nostrils flare and I can see the moment he realizes my precious queen's scent is staining my skin. His expression turns sympathetic and his voice drops slightly. "We have an incoming message from Queen Cassandra and her takadon."

Stalking over to a console, we answer their call. I see the shock jump onto Queen Cassandra's face when she sees the scene playing out behind me.

My voice is dull and hollow when I speak. "What are your losses, Queen Cassandra?"

It is her takadon, Mathadar, who answers. "We have lost three queens. Fortunately they did not make it to the hatchery. Tela was able to keep them from boarding her vessel entirely. The two smaller ships dropped behind us for protection and we were able to keep the enemy vessels from getting to it."

"I am relieved to know the younger queens were protected. I wish it had been so for our crew. The enemy managed to get three eggs and one of our human queens."

Mathadar leans forward and I can see he is affected by our loss. "I'm given to understand by Direk that one of the eggs was female. We believe that's why they attacked your vessel."

"Who are these aliens and what do they want with our females and young?"

"Their ship was recognized as belonging to the Moltan."

Direk quickly adds, "We found evidence of communications between them and the aquatics when we searched the aquatics' database on this ship. They are a reclusive species that inhabits this region of space. They rarely talk with other species, engage only in a limited amount of trade, and never show their faces. The few species that have traded with them report they talk over the coms with no visuals and exchange goods by drone."

"They've found a way to mask their appearance." I know that I'm stating the obvious but I wish to hear what Mathadar has to say on the subject.

"We believe they are cloaking their form by artificial means, but whatever they are using does nothing to mask their shadows. That's basically all we caught on our security feeds. They are tall, have strange headgear that looks almost like antlers of some sort, and move about on legs that bend in the opposite direction from humans and us. Our weapons are no match for theirs. Outside of that we know little."

I'm itching to deal death on all the Moltan. "Do we have any idea where they have gone?"

We're getting reports that the only trading partner they have in this area are the Sparloc. They are a highly advanced species with a small home base kept secret in this sector of space."

My interest surges. "They have a settlement nearby?"

Direk shakes his head, his horns slipping back. "It's more of a trading post than a settlement. The database indicates they have five large warehouses and a planetary defense grid. Such grids are virtually impregnable. Even if we manage to locate the planet, which is a remote possibility because they intentionally deleted the coordinates after each stop there, we would likely not be able to land because of the protective grid."

Pulling my data pad from my utility belt, I glance up at Mathadar. "Put all the information you have in the data stream. If we try hard enough, we may be able to search through their backups for a location. Every security system has a weakness. It will be my job to discover it."

Queen Cassandra's voice joins the conversation again. "Time is of the essence. It's likely they want the women for a specific purpose related to reproduction."

Mathadar chimes in his own gloomy thoughts. "They may wish them to test biological weapons."

Queen Cassandra gasps, clearly shocked by the thought of her soft human counterparts being used for such a nefarious purpose.

Mathadar tightens his wing around her as he speaks quietly. "It matter not what the enemy has in store for them. The fact remains that the longer the queens and little ones are held in captivity, the more likely it is the Moltan will succeed in whatever devious plan they've devised."

"I will waste no time in discovering a weakness that might be exploited to get my queen and the others back."

Mathadar's expression morphs into one of shock. It looks comical on his harsh features. Clearly he was not expecting me to be chosen. Even as I scroll through the information, a little voice in the back of my mind whispers the truth. I've not truly been selected to be Queen Daisy's permanent protector. Still, I feel in my soul that I've found favor enough in her eyes to believe she wants me for her own. For me, she is the only queen who will do.

Mathadar's pleased voice draws me from my straying thoughts. "Congratulations on being selected by a queen, Darnok. You are well worthy of the privilege."

"I am not flawed." Unsure why I said such a thing, my wings come up in an aggressive pose. Again, I'm not entirely certain what my own problem is. I shake my head, trying to get myself together. "I will contact you when I have a plan."

"We are all working on this together, Darnok. Add your thoughts and ideas to the stream. It's too important to be left to just one person."

"Agreed." I'm vaguely aware of the screen going blank as I continue scrolling through the information. Direk hovers over my shoulder. His words barely register in my quest to pick through all the details on our enemies I now have at hand. I murmur, "Gather every able-bodied warrior we have and draw down warriors from the other ships. When a plan is in place, I want them ready."

Direk's mouth falls open. "You heard Commander Mathadar. We are to work with the other ships, not take over this mission ourselves."

I turn on him, aggravated that he is arguing instead of obeying my commands. "My queen's life is in danger. I wait for no man or queen to gift me with permission to hunt down her abductors and deal them the grisly death they deserve."

"You sound more interested in getting revenge on your enemies than rescuing your queen."

My wings flare open and I feel my horns come to life. The sight of my aggressive stance sends Direk staggering back from me, his expression slack with terror. It's moments like this that I remember what a terrifying vision I must be to other warriors, being larger and possessing twice the wingspan of most of the others. "I do not know why you try to peck away at my control in this moment, but make no mistake, my friend. I will tear through any being who dares to stand between me and my queen. If you cannot or will not follow my lead, then move aside. Those are the only two options available to you."

Pharon's voice sounds off behind me. "He means no harm, Commander. Males without queens to protect can scarcely understand the clawing need to protect her. Direk is not wrong about who is leading this mission. It is not you."

I know better than they do. "You might wish to check with the queen and her takadon, for I seriously doubt she will risk her one and only male, the one carrying her young, on such a dangerous mission."

Pharon's head tilts slightly. "I did not think of that. You are most fit to lead after Commander Mathadar."

Direk pulls himself together and stands at attention. "I will liaison with the other ships and ensure your commands are carried out to the very last detail."

Looking from one to the other and then around at the assembled crew who have all stopped to witness the discord, I speak. "I care nothing for leadership or power. Once my queen is safely under my wing, let command duties fall to others. I care only for my queen."

Turning back to the small device in my hands, I know what they are all thinking. I can see it on their faces. They think Darnok had a queen and instead of staying at her side and protecting her, he ran off to secure the ship. Mathadar clearly stayed at his queen's side and Roan likely did the same. I alone failed in my duty. That's evidence of my poor judgment and makes me unworthy of being chosen by a queen. Pulling myself from morose thoughts, I turn my attention back to the task at hand.

14 ENGINEERING AN ESCAPE

DAISY

Being dragged through the enemy vessel feels all too familiar and is bringing up bad memories of being abducted by the aquatics. This ship is an elegant, state-of-the-art vessel, unlike the one I was held captive on before. The walls are made of some kind of composite metal that shifts and momentarily takes on an almost liquid quality when I accidentally fall into it. One of the huge beings tightens his grasp on my arm and jerks me back away from the wall. When I slam into a hard chest, it's one trauma too many and my vision slowly dims. My arms are too heavy to lift and when darkness overtakes me, I have the cold hard satisfaction of knowing I fought with everything I had. It's little consolation against the fact that I lost, but I'm still proud of myself.

I wake strapped to what I recognize as an alien healing platform. This one doesn't seem to be floating. I can tell because it has no give when I move. Restraints are holding my arms and ankles to the padded top. If it weren't for the restraints I'd swear I was back on Earth, lying on an exam table. Tugging gently on the restraints, I test them to see if I can pull free. It's a stupid thought. They wouldn't tie me to the table and foolishly allow enough slack for me to escape. That would defeat the whole purpose of restraining someone.

The minute they realize I'm awake, two of them rush over to me. They look much like the reptilians I once encountered while still on Earth. They're wearing white uniforms with clear plastic covers. The patch on their shoulder is one I recognize. While I was on Earth the government streamed videos of different alien races and their signs for medical units, hydration stalls, and restrooms. These beings are wearing the emblem for medical personnel.

I stare into their eyes as they begin scanning me and fussing over my readings. They have scales and large round dark eyes. Instead of eyebrows, there is a large ridge that arches over each eye, disappearing behind their flat ears. Shock tears through me as I realize they're scared. I can see the fear in their eyes and tell by their awkward, jerky movements. One keeps glancing over his shoulder and my eyes follow his to see what's scaring them so.

My lips press together in a firm line. All I see is a huge person-shaped shadow against the wall. He's bulky, and there's something about his head that isn't right. Maybe he's wearing a helmet or something because the shape of his head is large and elaborate. The alien makes a strange noise and the reptilians jump, moving quicker.

One whispers, "They're never going to let us go unless we figure out how to splice the human's genome with that of the Vithican."

The other hisses, "Shush. Don't let him hear you."

"They're asking the impossible."

"We need to figure it out or they'll kill us like they did

the others."

Vithican. I know that word. It's the term they use for the symbiont that infects all the young Draconian females with the parasites. Terror lances through my chest. Is it on this ship with me now? The last thing I want is to serve as a guinea pig for these reluctant reptilian scientists. I'm in vastly more danger that I thought. If the shadow aliens killed people to motivate these two scientists to perform some kind of gene-splicing experiment, they'll certainly kill all three of us once they've gotten what they want.

The shadow creature speaks again, his voice harsh and rough. It causes the scientists to panic again. I hear the door slide open and then the shadow is gone. The reptilians relax a bit.

"I am grateful we have a few moments to ourselves. I cannot organize my thoughts when the shadows are standing over me."

Speaking up, I point out the obvious. "Actually there was only one shadow."

The quiet one whispers, "They are evil spirits. Do not speak of them."

"Gee, aren't you a little superstitious for scientists?"

The first one speaks with a quiet dignity. "Forgive us, human. Vontel is overwrought because they killed the entire crew of our ship."

Vontel leans closer. "We are all that remains of the twelve-person crew of our scientific exploration vessel. I have no wish to join our crew in the hereafter."

Tugging at the wrist restrains, I announce, "I don't see any of us making it out of this situation alive. If they killed your whole crew, what are the chances they're going to let us go? You two can bear witness to the attack on your vessel, just as I can about the attack on our vessel."

Both of the reptilians freeze in place with equally shocked expressions on their faces.

"Look, they aren't going to leave eyewitnesses behind. That's not how crime works."

The first scientist makes a noise in the back of her throat that sounds like frustration. "The human is correct, Trexor. We were thinking there would be no reason to kill us if we did their bidding. Though our logic was sound, it's clear we were mistaken."

"There is no way off this ship. We threw everything we had at them in our first fight and had our entire crew at our back. We lost. It would be foolish to attempt to deceive them. They are likely listening to us, even now." Reaching out to cover Vontel's hand with his own, he speaks soothingly. "We must comply with their wishes for now."

Now I'm interested because they sound like a couple looking for a way out of the situation. That gives us common ground. They're probably right about the shadow freaks listening in on the conversation.

I decide to give it rest for now and keep my eyes and ears open. I already spied the eggs in a huge round incubation chamber across the room. They're sitting quietly soaking up the gentle lighting flowing down from above. It occurs to me that I have no idea how long it will be before they hatch. They're each about the size of a fist. Maybe they grow larger or just mature inside the shell. I'm ashamed of myself for not focusing on that part of the Draconian database. Hatchlings seemed like an issue I wouldn't have to deal with for a very long time.

As Vontel and Trexor labor over every readout and argue about how best to proceed with the gene splicing, my mind drifts back to Darnok. We were finally getting to know each other when the ship was attacked. I like how quickly he warmed up to me. I can almost feel his lips moving against mine in a kiss that started out tentative and ended rough and needy. He brought his wings up around me, sheltering me inside. It's warm, intimate, and smells like his body. A lot of women might be put off by that, but I really like being sheltered by him.

I also remember the tender way he drew out my orgasm and how he seemed to be in no hurry to satisfy that gigantic hard-on he was sporting. My body warms to the memory of his mouth on me. God, he's way too good at bringing me to climax that way. I loved every single thing about being with him. If I'd only followed his orders and stayed in my quarters, I could be enjoying his good company even now. Glancing across the room at the three eggs, I realize that I don't regret going to the hatchery. If not for that bold and foolish move, they'd be sitting here with no hope of being rescued. I know with certainty that we are going to be rescued. Darnok will come for us.

My mind wanders back over all the cute stuffed creatures he made for me. When the first one didn't turn out the way he expected, he just kept making them. That tells me he's not the kind of man to give up. It also makes me believe he will keep trying to find me.

Wiggling in an effort to break free of the ties holding my wrists to the table, the blanket shifts, exposing a breast. I hate that they removed my clothing at some point and covered me with this medical blanket. It's warm enough, but I have no idea where my lovely gown went. It grieves me to lose it because it was a gift from my dark defender. I can only pray he managed to stave off the attack before any other women were taken. I can't help but wonder if all the ships were attacked or just ours.

My stream of internal questions is answered soon

enough. The doors slide open and three hover boards are pushed through the door, each with a human woman lying unconscious on it. I crane my head to see if I recognize anyone. Though I can't see clearly, I don't recognize any of them.

The scientists rush over and begin tending to them. I can tell by the tone of their voices that they're horrified by their condition. I can only hear muffled snatches of their conversation. They're saying something about being malnourished and one is bleeding from her head.

I tear up, because my emotions are all over the place. I'm used to being restrained, so strangely enough that doesn't bother me. Being abducted again and seeing the other women brought in lying lifeless on the hover boards is a brutal reminder of what we've been through, and it seems never-ending. I'm beginning to feel like human women are just objects to be bought, sold, and used by aliens. The logical part of my brain knows that's not completely true, because the Draconians have been really nice to us. All the rest of the aliens we've met have been real asshats though.

I pull myself together about the time one of the women regains consciousness. She begins yanking at her restraints before screaming. "Oh, hell no. Not again. Get the fuck off me, you pricks."

I yell across the room. "Only one of them is a prick; the other is female."

"What the hell?" She lifts her head, blowing a thick lock of red hair out of her face. "Who the hell are you?"

"I'm a fellow abductee. You can probably tell because I'm tied to my exam table just like you are." Okay, that was unnecessarily snarky.

Her eyes drift up to my bound hands. "What the hell happened? I was in my room when all hell broke loose. The

emergency warning sounded and my door lock engaged."
Turning her attention to Vontel, she spat, "Stop poking me
with whatever that is."

I already guessed the purpose of the small metal prod.
"It's got a sensor on the end that probably takes your
temperature or something. Anyway, now you know what
happened. The ship was attacked and we ended up
abducted again."

"I've already decided that I'm not playing nice this
time."

"Same here, but you're harassing the wrong aliens.
Vontel and Trexor are abductees as well. The shadow aliens
killed their whole crew and keep threatening to kill them as
well unless they do some gene splicing with us and the Vithican creature."

"This day just keeps getting better and better. What's
your name?"

"Daisy Callahan."

Vontel and Trexor make a rough wheezing noise that I
suspect is laughter. I don't even have to ask, because my
translator is telling that my last name is suspiciously similar
to the word they use for refuse.

"My name's Stephanie Mercer. Don't worry, I won't
trash talk your name or anything like that."

"You're pretty funny for a girl tied to the damn bed."

Before I can answer an older female voice sounds off.
"Cut it out, both of you. We're in dire straits here and you
two fools are yakking it up."

Stephanie's contrite voice responds, "Sorry, Ma. We
were just trying to bring the tension down a little."

I'm quick to apologize as well. "I'm sorry as well, Ms.
Mercer."

"Any idea what's going on here?" There is a brief pause

and she adds, "I mean besides us getting abducted and Scaredy-cat One and Two being forced to gene splice us with a crazy Draconian parasite?"

"Well, they took four of us in all, all women, and killed I don't know how many Draconian men to get us. They also took three Draconian eggs. They're in an incubation unit on the far side of the room. I don't know how, but we need to get the hell off this ship before we come into contact with the parasite. If that thing infects us, it's game over."

The older woman clears her throat. "That's a little dramatic but nonetheless accurate. Do any of you have any ideas on how to get clear of this mess?"

Vontel hisses, "Quiet. They listen to our every word."

I open my mouth and lies pour out. "I was a doctor back on Earth. I'll help you with the gene splicing if you untie me."

Scaredy-cat One and Two are at my side within seconds. Trexor stares down at me intently as if trying to ascertain if I am telling the truth. His female sidekick seems a little more astute. "You will... help us ...if we untie you? You promise to keep your word?"

"I promise to help both of you and I never go back on my word." I'm totally sincere about that, and it comes through in the tone of my voice.

Trexor shakes his head but for some reason it looks more like the way a horse shakes its head than a human. "I do not think releasing the human is a sound idea."

Vontel lifts her head to look her partner in the eyes. "It is a good idea. Trust me about this, Trexor."

"We do not have permission..."

Vontel is already releasing the straps on my wrists. I manage to keep the smile off my face with supreme effort. She moves to the end of the platform and begins working on the straps holding my ankles. I touch the red band of abraded flesh that I'd rubbed raw by trying to escape. It's a good lesson in using my brain instead of my brawn.

I sling my legs over the side of the platform and notice it is securely bolted to the floor. Vontel pulls a fresh uniform out of a nearby cabinet and hands it to me. "The cleansing unit is the door on the right. Don't take too long. We have much work to do."

Nodding, I wrap the blanket around me and head to the door she indicated with the crisp clean uniform tucked under one arm. Though there's no mirror, I know I look like shit because of my reflection in the shiny metal wall. It takes me a minute to figure out how the shower works and I'm disappointed when it turns out to be a sonic shower or something along those lines. When I'm finished, I feel cleaner than I've felt in my life. Even my teeth and ear canals feel clean. I pull the uniform on, slipping my feet into the attached boots built into the end of each leg. It's not the best fit but I make do. Rushing out to the medical unit as quickly as possible, I approach the scientists.

After a short conversation, it's decided that I will work with Vontel to learn what all the equipment is used for so we can determine if we even have the necessary tools to perform the procedure they are demanding of us. I'm also on a mission to make note of what might be useful for an escape. The other women chat quietly amongst themselves. I think Ms. Mercer is clued in to why I'm cooperating so hard. The other two women have some choice insults for me and I'm not gonna pretend that doesn't hurt. It looks like it's up to Vontel and me to figure a way out of this situation. I stand tapping my nails on the console and it gives me an idea. I wonder if anyone aboard Cassandra's armada knows Morse code. I can't be the only Girl Scout of the bunch.

15 CLEVER QUEENS

DARNOK

I listen to the sounds we've picked up over the communication lines. It is difficult to think of this series of taps and pauses as a form of useful communication. Yet Roan insists that's exactly what it is.

His face is lit up with hope for the first time since my queen was taken. He's eagerly explaining everything to me. "At first we thought it was just random background noise, but my queen listened to it and believes it to be primitive Earth communication. It is a digital signal that doesn't degrade over time hidden as background noise inside the data stream used by the planets in this sector of space. My Meiko tells me that many Earth females participate in a paramilitary training program as small children."

It is the same with our people. Warriors are trained from a very early age. "They must have incompetent teachers, for none of the human queens are proficient at hand-to-hand combat."

"I am told they were not taught skills in battle." My eyes find his. "They learn wilderness living skills and are required stand on the street selling delicious confections."

"Thanks be to the gods that the human queens are afforded such training. Survival skills in the wild will certainly be useful when we claim a planet for our own."

Roan nodded his agreement. Gesturing to the information repeating on a loop on the screen in front of us, he continues. "This is the code our new queens utilized to communicate with home base in the event the enemy was spotted, they need to be resupplied with more confections, or medics are needed."

I'm fascinated by their ingenuity. "This is the first promising lead we've had since their disappearance three days ago." I've not slept the entire time, relying upon energy boosters to keep me awake and functional. Such is the way with our kind. Watching the screen I clearly see the pattern. "It appears to be referencing a point in space not far from our current coordinates." Turning to our navigator, I take a deep breath. "Direk, initiate a scan of that entire area immediately."

"Scanning, sir." Though he challenged me before, Direk is usually strictly formal when we are on the bridge. Even though he's prone to give me advice on queens when we're dining, he respects the chain of command. He's one of many good males who might end up giving their lives to secure the safety of our queens. My chest aches when I remember my former dining partner sacrificing himself in a vain effort to save my queen and the unborn hatchlings. When we retrieved the escape pods from the hatchery, the caretakers recounted how Queen Daisy and Elder Valden worked together to secure the safety of the little ones. Now he is gone and I am left grieving my friend and terrified for my new queen.

Direk's voice sounds off. "I'm not picking up a craft in orbit around the planet, sir."

"We need to proceed with extreme caution. Since the Moltan can cloak themselves, it's likely they can cloak their ships." I flip open a com channel and summon Queen Cassandra and Takadon Mathadar. I briefly explain our findings.

Queen Cassandra's face lights up. "Have Meiko formulate a quick response and proceed to the coordinates."

Mathadar says what we all know is solely for the benefit of his queen "We'll be able to scan the surface of the planet more thoroughly when we're closer. Picking up human bio-signs should be easy. We can also identify the bio-signs of any other aliens in our database. However, picking up the aliens responsible for the attack on our armada will be impossible since they were cloaked and did not show up on our internal sensors."

His queen responds wryly, "We'll just have to remember going into this situation that they are lurking in the shadows and be on the lookout for them."

Tugging his queen closer to his side, Mathadar contributes another suggestion. "I advise that if any of our teams are fortunate enough to uncloak one of them, we stop long enough to take a full body scan and send it immediately, along with visuals of their weapons."

Nodding, I murmur, "Agreed. I'm going to reflect the coordinates back in a single low-level soundwave. If this is a communication from my clever queen, she will be monitoring closely for a response from us."

"Do it, Darnok. We'll monitor your communications attempts while holding back in battle formation in case things go sideways."

Bowing my head slightly to Queen Cassandra, I can see the wisdom of her plan. If we converge on the planet and they engage with us, we'll risk hitting each other in an attempt to lock on to their cloaked ship.

When the screen goes black, I step closer to the communications console. Leaning over, Roan shifts over to give me access to his assigned station. My fingers fly over the controls as I mirror the signal back.

We wait several long minutes and another message comes through.

Roan perks up in his seat, his wings lifting in excitement. It only takes him a moment to shove the message through the translation program he designed. "She says there are three other women and three eggs. She's requesting a shuttle drop down with a contingent of warriors. She's identified an area on the far side of the planet where there is an anomaly in the configuration of the protection grid. Once we hit the lower atmosphere, we can take small hovercraft to their encampment."

"We lost many warriors during the last battle," Phan cautions from the doorway. "After losing on our own ship, what makes you think we can be victorious battling them on their own turf?"

Turning to face our resident medic, I frown at him. "Our queens and young need rescuing. It matters not at all our chances of victory. We must try."

Meiko appears in the doorway beside him and slips onto the bridge. "Daisy's smart. She wouldn't lure you there if there was no hope of winning."

My wings pick up and a smile tugs at the corners of my mouth. "I believe you are correct about Queen Daisy. I trust her with my life."

"I want to come with you." Meiko whirls around to face off with her sister. Before she can object, I deny Queen Aiko's command. "I must refuse your request,

Queen Aiko. This mission is too dangerous to risk more queens."

"It might have escaped your notice, but I'm a person as well as a queen."

"Queens are precious and must be protected at all costs."

Folding her arms over her chest, she shoots me a withering look. "Yeah, I've heard about how damned precious we are. In fact that's about all I've heard since you guys picked us up. Truth be told, I'm getting pretty sick of it."

"I have no wish to be disrespectful but arguing with you about obvious things is keeping me from the task at hand. Find another warrior to stroke your ego, for I have more important tasks to attend to at the moment."

Her mouth falls open, but before she can object her sister moves forward, rushing her from the bridge.

Roan's jaw locks and I can see the displeasure on his face. "You did not have to be rude to my new queen's kin."

Scanning through our crew roster, I choose warriors, armaments, and other various supplies for our mission to the Moltan vessel. "I have less interest in arguing the point with you than with Queen Aiko, Roan. Go console your queen and her sister, but leave me to the task at hand."

Coming to his feet, I see his horns slicked back and his wings tight against his back. "In your rush to save your queen, you go too far. Disrespecting a queen is treason. This ship belongs to her, not you."

Finally glancing up, I take a deep breath. Standing at full height, I lift my chin. "This ship belongs to the person who can lead. Need I remind you who that is?"

"It is you."

"For the moment, it is. Move aside, I beg you. Do not make an enemy of a friend this day."

Turning on his heel, he motions to a secondary crewmember to take his place. How this day went from bad to worse if beyond my ability to reason. Up is down and down is up. Friends are foes and distractions are keeping me from rescuing my queen. Don't they know that she's in terrible danger? Gods, I need her back on this ship, safely sheltered under my wings. I need her smiles, her laughs, and her soft touches. I need to be between her quivering thighs and to hear her screaming my name as she comes on my tongue. Not one of them understands my situation.

Just when I'm alienating the people closest to me and I'm beginning to think things can't get any worse, our security officer announces truly horrifying new information. "Commander Darnok, we're receiving a new encrypted transmission from Queen Daisy." There is a slight pause and his eyes find mine. The message states, "Vithican queen possibly on-site."

A cold chill creeps up my spine, settling at my wing base. The symbiont we attempted to kill is currently within striking distance of my queen. I bolt into action, intent on doing everything within my power to get to my queen before it is too late.

I look from the screen to Vontel. The language the Moltan speak is not in my translation program. For some reason they can communicate freely. Either they added their language to her translation program or the Moltan speak her reptilian language. I'm guessing humans are not important enough to merit that consideration.

Shooting me an anxious look, she speaks in a lowered voice. "Our captors are angry. They brought us to this outpost because we told them we didn't have the proper equipment to perform something as complex as gene splicing. Now that we have a relatively modern medical unit at our disposal they want rapid results. We are not meeting their expectations."

I mull over their concerns for a moment, trying to figure out a way to stall them. "Tell them we need to synthesize a treatment to stabilize the genome of the host once the genes are spliced. Otherwise, there will be a catastrophic cascade failure of their genome." Yeah, that sounds like a good lie. It'll work. It has to.

Vontel stares at me for a brief moment like I'm perhaps the most foolish creature in the entire universe. Honestly, I'm just making up crap and we both know it. Best case scenario is Vontel modifying my lie into something more believable.

Nodding slightly, she accepts the challenge. Taking a deep breath, she begins speaking. There are rapid bursts of speech and then some stuttering and the pace picks back up. Since her language is translated by my processor, I hear her giving some long, drawn-out, intricate explanation that's so far above my ability to understand that I kind of zone out.

We've done everything possible to enable Darnok to affect a rescue. Although Trexor was terrified to snoop around the Sparloc security system, he managed to sneak in using a key code we lifted from one of our guards. We've lied and schemed for the last five days. I just hope the Draconian warriors are still searching for us. I believe Darnok would not give up the search for me or the eggs easily, but the other warriors can be just as stubborn.

Finally, Vontel closes down the communications line. Turning to me, her expression is blank and her voice tight. "We are out of time, human." Anyone listening might think she means about the gene splicing. I know she means the danger has increased to the point that the Moltan might kill us because they're not buying our stall tactics.

Vontel and I stare at each other for a long moment before I speak. "We are close to a solution. Don't give up yet. There is still a chance we'll make it out of this alive."

She blinks first, her eyes darting across the room to Trexor. "I'm with child. Did you know that?"

Suddenly, my understanding of their situation takes a quantum leap forward. My hand comes out to grasp her arm, hoping to transfer some of my strength to her. "We're almost finished with this procedure," I lie. "I'll personally see you make it back to your people, safe and sound." That part's not a lie. No matter what happens, I've vowed to myself to see these two scientists and the others to freedom or die trying.

She looks down at my hand and lets out a shaky breath. "I believe you, human."

"Let's get back to work. For now, we need to give the solution to our little problem time to catch up with us."

She understands my cryptic words. We're just waiting for Darnok to come blasting through the door. Truth be told, it's all I think about. I eat, sleep, and dream about being rescued and how I'm never letting my sexy warrior out of sight ever again. I've spent my down time daydreaming about all the sexy things I'm going to do to him. They range from sheltering under his wing, to running my nose up and down his skin, enjoying his masculine scent, to worshiping him on my knees. God, the dirty thoughts just keep coming, no matter where I am or what I'm doing. Even in this place where we're forced to work on a project that might end the human race by splicing our genes with the Vithican parasites, Darnok is always in my thoughts.

A sick feeling twists in my gut, because I think they want to elevate the parasites to humanoid form. If they splice their genes into human women, they won't technically be parasites anymore. The Vithican part will be encoded in our DNA and passed on to our children genetically. Though I don't know why the Moltan are intent upon seeing this done, I can't deny it will elevate the Vithican species in ways simply existing at the expense of a host never could. In other words, what is good for them is damn near tragic for us.

We hear a commotion outside and my heart sings

because it sounds like battle. Grabbing Vontel, we run across the room to where Trexor is pretending to perform procedures on the elder Mercer. She's more tolerant of our little ruse than the other two women. They're both young and scream obscenities at us every time we get close. Since we're being monitored most of the time, I've tried to send subtle messages that things aren't what they seem and the elder Mercer has told them to pipe down more than once, but nothing gets through to them.

Since the gig's clearly up, we begin untying the others. The moment I release one of Stephanie Mercer's hands, she punches me right in the damned face. Pain explodes on one side of my face as she shouts, "That's what you get for being a fucking traitor to your own kind, bitch."

She gets me good and sends me staggering back a step or two. Thankfully, by that time Vontel has released her mother and is at my side. I cup my cheek protectively as I move my jaw back and forth.

Her mother leans over the table, shoving her roughly back down. "That's enough, Steph."

"The hell it is. She's been working with the enemy to turn us into hosts for those nasty parasites. Let me up. I'm gonna kill her with my bare hands."

Her mother grasps her shoulders and gives her a good shake. "Shut up and listen for a change, child. They've been trying to get us rescued and it worked." Her hands move to the restraints as she continues speaking. "I'm going to untie you but you better keep your hands to yourself, young lady."

Stephanie blinks up at her mother and for a brief second I can see her putting all the pieces of the puzzle together in her mind. She's no doubt thinking of our whispered conversations, numerous hissed disagreements, and general lack of cutting anyone open. Her eyes narrow and I get the feeling she's still torn between believing her mother and thinking we're pulling one over on her.

Meanwhile, Trexor has released the other women and is securing the eggs. I walk over and the others follow. "I hope we're winning the battle outside."

Vontel grabs a handheld healing unit and begins to use it on my cheek. Stephanie's still shooting me suspicious looks, though I can tell her mother isn't going to let her escalate again. I honestly like Ms. Mercer. Her no-nonsense approach to surviving in captivity has made our situation easier to bear.

The remaining woman is standing off to the side with her arms wrapped around her stomach. She's told us her name is Hallie Patterson and she was taken while traveling from one remote city to another in the Northern provinces. She's been extremely anxious and quiet but her eyes seem to be everywhere, taking in all the details the rest of us might be missing. I'm just praying we get rescued today.

Trexor begins pacing. "I should be out there, defending my mate." I'm surprised, because I've been thinking of him as a nerdy scientist, not a fighter. The reality slams home that he's probably both, but he couldn't take a chance on fighting an unwinnable battle.

Vontel snaps the healing unit closed and closes the distance between them in three steps. When they're standing face-to-face, I realize something. They're perfectly matched for size, intelligence, and they are both scientists. Even their strengths and weaknesses balance one another. In the areas she's weak, he's strong and vice versa. I can see that their coloring is complementary. They're going to make beautiful babies. It makes me think that maybe a lot more goes into their mating choices than meets the eye. It seems kind of odd to find they take so many details into consideration when selecting a mate. Then I wonder if they even select their own mate or is it an arranged marriage? Maybe they genetically match males and females for breeding purposes. I vaguely remember that one species of aliens did this but I can't remember if it's the reptilians. The more I think about it, the more pieces of the puzzle click into place.

Suddenly, there is a loud blast and a gigantic hole appears in the wall on the other side of the room. Darnok steps through the cloud of smoke and dust. He looks amazing and battle worn. My clit tingles at the sight of him. He came for me. I thought he would but here he is. Before I know it, I'm running across the room to him. His eyes light up and he moves to meet me halfway. When I'm a few feet away, I launch myself at him, vaguely aware that more warriors are pouring in through the hole and moving around us.

I land against his chest and almost choke on the smoke that dusts up from him. He's dirty, dusty, bloody, and sweaty but it doesn't keep him from folding his wings around me. Inside the shelter of his wings there's only the two of us.

"You came."

"You knew I would."

"I hoped you would. There's a difference."

"You are my queen."

He doesn't elaborate and I realize that in his world, that says it all.

"You're my everything in the world that matters." Maybe I overstated that a little. Those eggs matter. Freedom matters. The other women matter. In my mind, Darnok is the most personally important thing in my life. He seems to know what I mean because he pulls me closer, and a smile tugs at the corners of his mouth. "I will be your protector, your lover, and your companion for as long as you see fit to keep me."

"How does forever sound?"

He lets out a tired laugh. "It sounds like a very long time, my queen."

"To me it doesn't sound like nearly long enough."

His expression turns serious. He leans his forehead against mine. "It is my honor to serve."

A loud abrasive voice cuts through our joyous reunion. "Can you two lovebirds give it a rest? We're in some peril here."

It's Stephanie, because who else would it be? With a long-suffering sigh, Darnok drops his wings and I turn in the direction of the complaining voice. I jerk in his arms when I see the warriors have surrounded Vontel and Trexor and are pointing weapons at them. I lurch forward. Trexor has Vontel sheltered behind his slightly larger body and is baring his fangs and softly hissing a warning to the Draconians. I've never seen him behave this way before and it's a little shocking.

"Don't shoot. They're not working with the enemy. They were abducted from their ship and forced to work for the Moltan."

Darnok's cautious voice sounds off behind me. "Are you certain, my queen?"

"I'm certain. They helped me get a message out to you by breaking into the data stream. The crew of their science vessel was killed and they were taken hostage."

With a swift jerk of his chin, the warriors all reluctantly

holster their weapons. I quickly tell them all about how the Moltan wanted them to splice DNA from the Vithican queen with human DNA and how we tricked them into thinking we were complying with that request long enough to get a message out.

Darnok is still standing behind me and his arms tighten around me, drawing me back against his chest. "Secure the queens and the hatchlings. Search every dark corner for the Moltan and the Vithican queen."

Vontel speaks up in a shaky voice. "I don't think you'll find the creature here. They gave us biological samples to work with. Though we didn't open the seal, it appears to be tissue samples."

"Where are they? Tell us; do not approach the samples." My overprotective warrior's voice is deep and angry.

I have to admit to feeling a bit freaked out to find I've been in such close proximity to biological matter that could have found its way into my body and taken over my mind. I know this fear is not lost on Darnok.

It is Trexor who speaks. "Behind the third wall panel to the left is a stasis unit. Inside you will find three sealed canisters."

Darnok's arms drop away and he moves over to open the stasis unit. Vontel's voice rings out. "The canisters were designed to house particularly virulent and dangerous biological samples. Each one has a built fail-safe mechanism to incinerate the sample. If you wish I can activate the destruction sequence and destroy the parasite."

Darnok reaches for one of the canisters and I panic. "Please let Vontel do it. She's familiar with the procedure." I don't want him to get infected.

His hand freezes in midair and he looks over at me. He

must recognize the desperate look in my eyes because his hand drops to his side. Stepping back, he gestures for Vontel to move forward. "Hold it up so we can see everything you do." There's no need for him to issue any stern warnings, because we all know the Draconian warriors will drop her where she stands if she dares to double-cross them or anything like that.

We watch her pull on heavy gloves before turning to the containment unit. She gingerly lifts one the canisters into the air. It's about as long and round as my forearm and appears to be made of glass. It has a small white piece of tissue clearly visible. Somehow, it's just floating around in the canister though there's no fluid inside.

Lifting it over her head, she turns a large copper-colored disk built into the bottom. It seems like the destruction sequence is controlled by some kind of combination, because she turns it a full turn and then a quarter turn back and so forth. Finally, there is a loud click and she quickly sits the container down on a metal table and backs away.

There is a burst of light and we watch as the tissue sample catches fire and literally burns away until there is nothing but ashes. Vontel picks it up, shakes it to verify that there's nothing but ash inside, and then opens the top and adds three squirts of liquid from a brown bottle. After shaking it up, she repeats the same combination of turns on the copper disk. When she sits it down the liquid sizzles and kind of evaporates. The basic law of matter states nothing can be created or destroyed, it can only change forms. Whatever was in that bottle is now vapor. That's the only logical explanation.

We stand by silently and watch as she performs the same process for the remaining two containers. When it's over we breathe a collective sigh of relief. Only for my ever-overprotective warrior I worry that it may never be over. He turns to several of his men. "Quarantine this building until our healers can be brought down. I want it scanned thoroughly for any trace of hidden Vithican biological samples."

A tall Draconian warrior with deep purple skin bows his head. "I will see it done, Commander."

Giving the room one final suspicious look around, Darnok wraps one wing around me and leads me to the door. I can hear the others chattering as they move along behind us, flanked by several other crew members. The sun hits me in the face, reminding me that I've never seen this planet during the day. The building we were in had no windows and we arrived at night.

Stepping out of the artificial light and into the sunshine, I feel revitalized. A weight has been lifted from my shoulders. I don't even care that the ground is littered with the bodies of our captors. Nothing can distract from the elation of being free from the threat of death and knowing the Vithican samples have been destroyed. My dreams had been filled with nightmares of being infected by the parasites. Thanks to Darnok and the other Draconian warriors, we can now rest easy.

Stealing a glance at Darnok's scarred face, I ask curiously, "Are we going back to the ship?" Then I feel stupid. Where else is there to go except back to our ship?

"We are to remain on this planet until our healers can verify we are free from contamination by the parasite, my queen." It's common knowledge that males can't be infected with the parasite, so that means they don't want us potentially carrying the virus up to the ships and contaminating the other women.

"That makes good sense. It is safe here?"

His head tips down and his eyes find mine. "We eliminated the enemy; however, the Moltan vessel escaped intact. We cannot trust their machinery to scan properly for the parasite. It may have been tampered with."

I nod, realizing what he says is likely true. The Moltan are clever and controlling. It makes sense that there would be some redundancy built into their efforts to create a Vithican/human hybrid. "I see."

"I have secured a private shuttle for your use. The others are being cared for in a similar fashion. We will cleanse, dine, and wait for the healers to bring their scanning equipment down. Once you are cleared we will return to the ship."

"Don't you have duties to attend to down here?" I notice a ton of Draconian men milling about, clearing away bodies and making repairs on shuttles, equipment, and buildings.

"From this moment forward, my only duty is to keep you safe." His voice is pinched with sadness, pain, and what sounds like regret. I don't like to see him beating himself up about the situation.

He leads me onto a huge shuttle and into a well-appointed suite in the back. The moment the door shuts, I turn to him. "So what's the plan? Are you just going to follow me around like Mathadar does Cassandra?"

He freezes in place. "I would never presume to think of myself as your takadon." The moment the words slip from his mouth, I know that's what he wants more than anything in the 'verse. I know what a takadon is. The Draconian equivalent of a husband, bodyguard, best friend, and breeder all rolled into one. His eyes drift closed and he turns his head away slightly, taking a small step back. I hate that his wings are drooping to the point that they're almost touching the floor. My sexy, sweet, fierce warrior is more than sad. He almost looks humiliated. The next words out of his mouth let me know why.

"You have my apologies for failing to protect you, Queen Daisy."

"What are you talking about? You just rescued me?"

"Both Roan and Mathadar stayed with their queens and in doing so kept them safe."

Shock rolls through my gut, followed quickly by white-hot anger. "Explain."

His eyes lift to mine and I see the full depth of his misery. "They stayed sequestered with their queens. I left your side to fight the battle. You were taken because I was not there to protect you. I'm unworthy of being..."

My feet begin moving without conscious thought and suddenly I'm standing face-to-face with him. "I would never have been taken if I'd remained in my quarters like the other women. They took those of us they found wandering around the ship."

"I could have stopped them."

"Valden couldn't stop them. There were too many of them for any single warrior to have fought off, even one as powerful as you." Everything I've said is the truth and I need him to hear it.

My male is stubborn though. His expression closes off. "We will never know because I left you without a protector."

I struggle to explain how wrong he is in a way he'll understand. I don't like speaking ill of his friend Roan, but I can't stop myself. "Roan and Mathadar are selfish cowards. When enemies came knocking, they hid behind locked doors with their women and let you do the fighting for them."

His mouth falls open and even his tail goes still. I can

tell by his expression he's dumbfounded by my bold statement. The ridge running across his eyes dips into what I
recognize as a frown. His wings are all cockamamie, with
one slightly higher than the other. I've never seen that
before.

17   FALLING INTO LINE

DARNOK

Her words feel like a gut punch I wasn't expecting. Is that truly how she sees Roan and Mathadar, as cowards who hide when there is a battle to be fought? It seems too fantastical to be true that she doesn't understand how important she is in the general scheme of things.

"You do not understand, Queen Daisy."

Her expression turns even angrier. "Don't call me that. You called me your queen before and I got used to thinking of myself as yours. Don't you dare go back on your word now that the battle's won." She reaches out, placing both her hands on my chest, igniting a raging fire in my blood. Her voice drops to a whisper. "The only thing that got me through these last few days was believing that you'd come for me and in the end we'd be together."

My wings come out to wrap around her, drawing her close. She comes willingly into my arms, and I know complete joy. Nothing compares to having her eyes on me and her delicate hands smoothing over my body. I need this so much more than I've ever needed anything before. But I can't escape the cold hard fact that I failed her. "You need someone with better judgment..."

Fisting my uniform top in her hands, she interrupts, "I need *you*."

Something in my chest relaxes. "Knowing you were at the mercy of our enemies tore a gigantic hole in my soul. I will never make that mistake again, my queen." I murmur the last few words against her hair as I nuzzle the side of her head against my face.

Pulling back, some of the harshness ebbs from her expression. "You still don't understand. You were the only one with a queen who did the right thing."

"I'll admit to being totally lost at this point."

"What if every warrior on this ship had a queen to protect and they all stayed locked in their quarters?"

"Luckily that was not the case. Males who have been chosen stay with their queens leave the fighting to unattached males. It is our way."

Her voice hardens again. "Not anymore. From now on the most competent warriors engage the enemy and the least competent protect the queens and hatchery."

"That makes a certain kind of sense, but what if a queen's takadon falls in battle? That would harm the emotions of a queen."

Her hand reaches up to cup the side of my face. She looks right past my scars to see the real me. "You're in the Naxis now. Earth has millions of women looking for mates. Every single male who falls in battle was destined to be some queen's takadon."

Her words begin to sink in. "You demand that we utilize the strongest and most effective battle strategy, thinking it will result in fewer casualties among the warriors."

She nods. "On Earth we call it working smart as well as

hard. There are too few Draconians in this sector of space. If we are serious about founding a new home world, we'll need every single one."

"I must admit that it bothers me when an unmated male dies because his whole line dies with him." I see a slight smile tug at her lips. "You are wise beyond your years, my pale beauty."

"So, you'll take my words to heart?"

Drawing her closer, I dip my head respectfully. "I will speak with Queen Cassandra and make Mathadar understand our stance. Are you certain you are not angry with me for leaving your side in battle?"

"On the contrary, if you'd tried to stay locked in my quarters with me, I'd have lost respect for you as a protector. You have a responsibility to protect my ship, all the others, and especially the hatchlings. If I hadn't been captured and figured out a way to get a message to you, the other women and those little ones would have died badly. I'm more than satisfied with the way things turned out."

Now that she has spoken her mind, I see how intelligent she really is. "Queens were meant to lead. Where you lead, I will follow, my precious queen."

She grabs the collar of my uniform and drags me down for a human kess. It's long and sweet and filled with all the excitement that only a queen can bestow upon a male. When she draws back, I'm in awe of her. From this moment on my hearts beat only for this one queen. She alone saw through my scars. None of the others see the wisdom of my decisions. Only this soft, fierce queen knows my true worth.

When she pulls back, I smile down at the dreamy expression on her face. I do that to her: make her warm, happy, and satisfied. Her next words catch me off guard, though they shouldn't come as any great surprise.

"Will you be my takadon, Darnok?"

"I know deep in my soul that I am worthy of you."

"Is that a yes or no?"

Grabbing her up in my arms, I twirl her around in a circle. It's a wildly irreverent liberty to take with a queen, but mine laughs and allows her long arms to drift above her head. It's a carefree posture and I love seeing her like this. "I say yes to being your primary male."

Her hands land on my shoulders and she stares down at me. "Only male, not primary male. I only want you."

Nodding, I agree. "For now it will just be you and me."

Cupping my face in her hands, she sighs. "I want it to be just the two of us, forever and always. No other males are welcome in my bed."

"Like Cassandra and Mathadar?"

She nods, "Except he's a coward and you're a hero."

I can't help but laugh at her harsh judgment of Queen Cassandra's takadon. Then I realize that she just called me her hero. My throat closes with emotion. I bring her down, holding her close to my chest.

Before I can speak, our door chime sounds. Holding her close, I voice prompt the door open. Pharn enters to see my queen's arms wrapped around my waist. He's pulling a hover board with a medical scanner built into it.

"Greetings, Pharn. You may set the unit up on the far side of the room." Turning to my queen, I remind her of our plan. "Pharn is here to perform the medical scan we talked about."

"Let's get it over with, so we can spend some one-on-one time celebrating."

Pharn motions us over with a smile. "Are you celebrating being rescued?"

My queen laughs as she jumps onto the hover board.

"Though that's actually worthy of celebration, I'm more in the mood to celebrate Darnok agreeing to become my takadon."

Pharn freezes for a split second, but his expression gives no clue as to whether he approves of our joining. He begins the scan and steps back to let it run its course. "Are you interviewing secondary males for your family unit?"

Before she can manage a reply, I find myself speaking. "My queen wishes for only one male. Our joining will be as Cassandra and Mathadar."

Turning to me, the healer gives me a long thoughtful look before speaking. "Congratulations, my friend. You are well worthy of being chosen."

I can tell he's disappointed. Perhaps he was hoping to join with her. I should feel angry about another male wishing to breed for my queen, but I find myself feeling empathy for him instead. Nothing is more hopeless than knowing you will never serve a queen for your long life. Such was my life before I met my beautiful queen.

My sweet new mate must sense it was well, for she offers him encouraging words. "I want you to pay special attention to one of the rescued queens, Healer Pharn. Her name is Hallie Patterson. She's quiet and withdrawn. I think all the warriors frighten her. She needs someone to speak with her regularly and make sure she's well cared for because I don't think she will speak up to get her own needs met."

Pharn's head snaps around to gaze at her. "Are you saying this queen needs a male like me?"

"You're a healer and you have a nice bedside manner. Maybe you can get her to talk about whatever's bothering her. I'm sure she'd appreciate the extra support."

I watch as he stands a little taller and his wings lift. "It would be an honor to look out for your friend queen. Thank you for vesting me with this responsibility. I won't let you down, Queen Daisy."

"I knew that I could count on you, Pharn. How's my scan looking?"

"It's almost finished and there is no sign of contamination by the parasite."

"That's good news."

When the scanning beam comes to a complete stop, my queen comes flying back into my arms. Having her slight soft body sheltering under my wing feels more right than anything I've ever experienced. Pharn can't get out of the room fast enough. Looking down at her, I swallow thickly. "Thanks for directing him to seek out your friend queen."

Grinning impishly up at me, she laughs. "I thought for sure you were going to chide me for my little impromptu attempt at matchmaking."

Kissing the top of her head, I inhale her scent. "You gave him hope when he had none. No Draconian male would see that as anything other than compassionate."

"This may come as a complete surprise to you, but I don't want to talk about the healer. I want to talk about us."

Her expression is so open and adoring that I can't help but tease her a bit. "Oh no, you and I are settled business. You asked me to be your takadon and I accepted. You are not permitted to change your mind."

She snorts a laugh. "As if that would ever happen in a million years"

"Good. I wish to put my mouth on you again."

Her cheeks turn slightly pink. I find that charming. She shakes her head, denying me her sweet nectar. It makes me wonder if I have done something wrong.

"It's my turn to give you a special treat for agreeing to be mine."

"It's sweet that you wish to reward my compliance, but know that I wish nothing more than to be with you."

"If that's true, you're easy to please."

I feel my warrior's face slip, replaced by a smile I can't seem to control. "I like that you speak to me as an equal."

"We're about as equal as any two people can be, except you're handsome with all those bulging muscles and I'm a little on the plain side."

I chuff out a hoarse laugh. "You jest with me, my queen. Compared to your loveliness, I am the stuff of nightmares."

Her eyes lift to mine again. "What? You're all rough and tumble, like a man should be."

I can see from the expression on her beautiful face and her earnest tone that my new mate believes the words coming out of her pretty mouth. My spirit soars to know she does not think of me as a monster.

18 MATING

DARNOK

I step back, holding one hand out to her. "Come my queen, allow me to assist you in cleansing and then I will see you properly fed."

Her face lights up. "Thanks, I'd love to share a cleansing with you."

She assumed I meant for us to cleanse together. I forgot human queens do that. I force my face into a blank expression, lest I frighten her with the strength of my desire to see her naked with tiny trails of water dripping down her precious body. Since the queens have come under our wing, we have worked at modifying our ships and shuttles to suit their needs. Warriors are accustomed to using misters to clean our bodies, but our queens prefer water that rains down from above. I made sure the shuttle I selected was one that had been modified for the needs of a queen.

Drawing her under my wing once more, I take her to the cleansing unit. She stands, quietly watching as I make preparations. Having had little time to prepare, I ordered generic items our warriors had fabricated for the general population of queens aboard our vessel.

When I turn around, my tail stills and my wings unfurl in surprise. My queen has removed all her clothing in anticipation of cleansing and her body is just as beautiful as I remember it being. She's all pale flesh and soft curves. The blushing tips of her breasts are just as lovely as the tender seam of her sex, with a hint of pink flesh peeking out for me to see.

Shock tears through me when she steps forward and tugs at the seam of my uniform. When it opens, she pushes it back off my shoulders and her delicate hands skate across the planes of my chest. Her eyes are admiring all that I am and for once I do not feel as though I am lacking.

My hearts still in my chest when she goes quietly to her knees in front of me. Seeing her kneeling before me reminds me that she called me her king. Draconians do not have kings, only queens. Yet, here she is, on her knees in a worshiping pose. Though it is perversion of the highest order, I want this more than I have ever wanted anything in my life.

Grasping the uniform now hanging loose around my waist, she pulls it down. I panic, because if she does not stop my hard cock will be in danger of breaking free and slapping her in the face. My hands go to hers, stilling them.

"What you seek to reveal will not be pretty, my queen. Let me tend to you as a male should attend to the needs of his queen." It's a warning and she understands. I can tell because her expression shifts to one of annoyance.

"Do not deny me the opportunity to reward my new takadon, especially after he just rescued me from a fate worse than death."

I move my hands to sift through her soft strands. The humans call it hair and I love the way it slides through my fingers. Tilting her head back, I speak the words I know she wishes to hear. "Do with me as you will, my queen. I gladly accept the reward you seem too eager to bestow upon me."

My acquiescence seems to please my sweet queen. Her genuine smile breaks the cold vise I've kept clinched around my heart for so many years. I still beneath her touch, not looking forward to her reaction when she comes face-to-face with my huge, throbbing, scarred cock.

She tugs again and the uniform slides down my legs. She keeps pulling until I am obliged to step out of the built-in boots. Nothing could have prepared me for what she does next. Rather than giving me a visual inspection the way Draconian queens were wont to do with their selected mates, she takes my ugly cock in her hands and strokes up and down, sparking pleasure along the length of my pole. My head falls back and I groan. This is a reward I never thought to wish for from a queen. It makes me want to rescue her every day of our long lives.

I look down, enjoying the sigh of her serving me. She leans over and kisses the tip of my cock head, getting my precum on her lips. Though feeling her lips on me was amazing, I hate that she soiled herself like that. I freeze in place when her tongue comes out to run along the length of her lower lip. Then she repeats the obscene gesture with her top lip. I'm bizarrely fascinated by her dedication to cleaning her lips of my seed.

Just when I think she is clean once more, she leans over and runs the flat of her tongue around the head of my cock. This time, she doesn't pull back. She settles in licking over and around my cock, tracing the long scars and veins down to the base. I thought the salacious kess she placed on my cockhead was my reward, but now I can see it is a dance of her tongue over my sensitive flesh. It is the most pleasure I have ever known and that it is a gift from my humble queen makes it all the more meaningful.

If I thought to have figured out my new queen, I am proven wrong once more. The long languid strokes of her tongue were just a prelude to even more pleasure it seems. Her mouth closes over the end of my cock and she sucks. My eyes roll back into my head with pure searing pleasure. Her hands work in tandem with her mouth, creating a maelstrom of sensation zipping back and forth between my cock and stomach. My balls grow heavy, filling with my seed, and the thought of her sucking it down her throat almost makes me spill without permission.

One hand drops to her shoulder. "Stop now, my queen. I will spill..."

Her hands slide up to my hips and she holds me in place. That's the moment I realize her intent is to have me spill in her mouth. It's such a dirty, depraved thing to do to such a beautiful queen. Knowing she wants me this way chains my soul to hers. Her mouth slides down my cock as she tries to gobble more and more of my length. The moment she chokes herself, I lace my fingers through her pale strands and force her head back. She submits beautifully to my authority, subverting her will to my own.

I rock my hips back and forth across her tongue and she not only allows it but her hand drifts between her legs to toy with the tiny nub that brings her pleasure. To know she is so excited to have my cock in her pretty mouth that she can't help but touch herself is heady stuff for one such as me.

She swirls her tongue around the tip of my cock as the cleanser fills with the scent of her desire. It's too much. I was barely hanging on before but now my cock is spilling in the warm, soft confines of her mouth. My eager new queen swallows it down, sucking to make sure she gets all that she deserves.

I tug myself from her mouth and lift her into my arms. When I speak, my voice is low and rough. "Thank you, my queen. No warrior ever had such a fine reward."

Looking at her lovely mouth, I wish to make the human kess with her, but I don't know if she would consider that an attempt to take back some of the seed clinging yet to her lips.

Instead I step into the cleansing unit and allow the warm water to spill over our bodies. That's when I see her hand is still between her legs, leisurely stroking over her tender flesh. That will never do. Using my wings, I lift her up and splay her legs across my face. Using one hand, I pull her hand away and replace it with my mouth.

Her reactions to every place it touched when last I was between her thighs is seared into my mind for all time. I intentionally hit the highlights, knowing she desperately needs her first orgasm of the night. Sucking on her nub, much like she did my cock, I have her ready to scream my name in moments. Instead of pushing her over the edge, I vary my technique to keep her on the edge. Finally her breathless voice begins to beg. "Please let me come." I drive my tongue into her center, where her scent is the strongest. "Oh God, please." Pulling back I plant one finger over the tight rosette of her rear and press, even as I suck the tender bundle of nerves. She wiggles, trying to get me to let her have her way.

A streak of cruelty I never knew I had burns hot and strong in my gut. I hold her perfectly still, making her take my tongue. Truth be told, I love hearing her beg for release. Desperate to own her heart and all her sexual pleasure, I decide there and then that if I allow her come at all, it will be on my cock. Her legs begin to quiver and I know she's close to exploding.

I slide her down my front and slowly impale her on my waiting cock. Her eyes get big as I take my time rocking into her lush softness, each time going a little deeper. I feel something pop when I slide in deeper and a small cry breaks from her lips. Panic lances through my chest for a second before I remember the data stream documented many aspects of mating with a human queen. One of the things I learned was about was breaking the queen's virginal barrier. It is to be done with one's cock not one's fingers.

Smug satisfaction sets in when I realize I am her first and only male. My cock is the only one she will ever know. I know this makes me a bad male, because we are not supposed to be selfish and territorial about our queens. Yet I am feeling fiercely protective and territorial of mine.

She wiggles on my cock, making herself right at home. I can't keep the smile off my face for anything. I truly love this small queen with all my heart and soul. In this moment I understand why some of our males become so obsessed with their queens. It is because to have a queen means much more than a male being able to continue their line. Queens give a male purpose in life, for he becomes a protector. It also guarantees him tenderness, caring, and thus far unimaginable sexual pleasure. I would trade this for nothing in the 'verse.

When I look down into her pretty face, she moves to make the human kess with me, murmuring, "You smell amazing." The pride growing in my chest doubles because she is aroused by my mating scent. I know the breeders have powerful and alluring mating scents, but I never thought mine was fit to draw a queen. It seems that was mistaken. I've never been happier to be proven wrong.

"It's my mating scent. It's an evolutionary advantage meant to lure our mate to us while driving other males away."

Running her nose along my neck, she murmurs, "Well, it's working like a charm. I can't get enough of it." She drops delicate fluttering kesses down my neck and onto my chest before whispering, "Move, handsome. I'm eager to feel the pleasure you give."

I lean back slightly, eager to see our joining with my own eyes and freeze. The water drizzles over my shoulders and though I know it is warm, my skin ices over. My heart is a heavy stone sitting in my chest, for I have injured my lovely queen. Staring at the blood paining the lips of her sex, I am horrified beyond belief. Even my cock is smeared with her precious blood. Pulling out, I set her on her feet and begin to kneel.

Her hand reaches up to grasp one of my horns. "What's wrong? Don't you want me?"

"I don't deserve a queen. In my haste to have you, I have damaged your body."

Looking down, she gives an irritated growl. "I'm not injured."

"There is much more blood than there should be." Though she is not gushing by any stretch of the imagination, I think there should certainly be less.

She grabs the sprayer and begins cleaning every trace of the blood away. "Human women are all different. Some have very thin hymens that break when we engage in moderate exercise. Others have varying degrees of thickness, resulting in different amounts of bleeding. Some are so thick they must be pierced by a healer." Her face turns pink as she continues. "I know seeing blood is probably disgusting when you're trying to have sex, but it only happens the first time."

Stepping forward, I allow her to clean my cock as well. Knowing she is well causes my cock to surge again under her touch. Tilting her chin up, I gaze into her eyes, noticing how her eyes skitter away. "Nothing about you could be described as disgusting, my queen. You have my apologies for drawing attention to your one weakness."

Suddenly, she's laughing again. "My one weakness? You've got to be kidding me." Hanging the sprayer back up, she murmurs, "You're too much."

I hit the drying cycle and it takes but a moment for the moisture to evaporate from our naked bodies. Watching the droplets of water growing smaller and finally disappear altogether makes my cock throb with need. Her eyes drift down my body and back up again, taking in every detail and scar. I refuse to squirm like a hatchling under her scrutiny, so I go still once again. My face burns with shame but do not move by pure strength of will alone.

When the drying cycle completes, I follow her out of the shower, relieved she is well and voiced no complaint about my scarred body. Perhaps she realizes the body of a true warrior is nothing special to behold. She appears to accept me as I am, but I make a mental note to avoid subjecting her to the sight of me nude in the future.

She climbs onto the bed on all fours and my mouth falls open in surprise. I can see everything a warrior dreams of gazing upon between her legs. Her soft folds are even lovelier than I remember. She's small, pink, and delicate. Memories rise in my mind of having my mouth just there and I recall how delicious she tasted on my tongue.

Does she wish me to mount her from behind? Is that why she is on her hands and knees? I move forward with the intent to do exactly that when she turns and falls onto her back. I come to a stop, unsure of what she wishes, but she immediately spreads her legs in an almost inviting manner. I shuffle forward and she circles her legs around my hips and I come down on top of her, careful not to drop too much of my weight onto her.

Wrapping her hands around my horns once more, she pulls me up until I am face-to-face. Her gaze drops down to my lips and I make the human kess with her as she strokes my horns. Her hands on me sparks a kind of lust I've never known.

When the tips of her breasts graze my chest, I break the kess to investigate her body. When we were last together, her gown covered her there and I could not see the gentle slope of her breasts and the way her waist curves inward.

Now, I not only gaze at her rounded globes, I touch and squeeze before toying with the pretty decorative pink points. She's soft everywhere except the tips. They're hard and pointing right at me. Sucking one into my mouth, I swirl my tongue around the firm point, much like she did my cock earlier. That earns me a small needy noise from the back of her throat. I try different techniques and before long she is squirming beneath me and her hand attempts to slide down between her legs.

Grasping her wrist gently, I tell her, "Do not touch yourself, my queen. You will get only the pleasure I see fit to give."

Twisting her wrist from my grasp, she moves down again. Only this time she grasps my cock and gives it a long languid stroke. My eyes fly up to hers and I can see she is intent on having her way with me. This idea pleases me to no end.

I trail kesses down to the tiny nub between her legs and

lick her as I did before she was abducted by the Moltan. Her throaty cries of pleasure spur me on. When I suck the tiny nub into my mouth, she goes wild beneath me and comes screaming my name.

She's ripe for mounting but I hesitate, not wishing to cause her harm where she is raw from the breaking of her barrier. Her hands land on my cock again and her legs wrap around my waist tighter. She drags me forward and aims me toward her core.

I know it's wrong, but I can't give over this much control. In this moment I feel as though I must prove myself a worthy mate. Brushing her hands away, I slide one finger inside her warm body, thrusting a few times, and then I add another. Searching her face, I find nothing but pleasure. Perhaps it is as she said and the blood is no indication of injury.

Rubbing my cock against her wetness, I coat myself in her nectar before sliding the length of my cock over the nub that brings her pleasure. She jolts forward, and I thrill to sound of my name on her lips once more. When I move my cock down to her center, she moves forward slightly, as if to hurry me along. This beautiful queen wants my cock. I am not breeder, yet she desires me above all others. It takes a moment for that to settle in. Pride swells in my chest. My new queen has made me her takadon and she wants my cock. Whether it's for breeding or pleasure, I care not.

Rocking into her body a little at a time, I find myself able to go deeper with each thrust into her welcoming body. I feel more connected and secure about our bonding with each stroke. My heart and my head need this as much as my body does.

Mating a queen is the most pleasurable sensation known to my kind. She's just as lost in the pleasure as I am.

I look down to see her practically dancing on my cock. She's moving her hips, touching my stomach, and pulling me forward with her legs. I love everything about this encounter with my queen. I've never felt so desired. Thrusting in and out of her tight sleeve, I feel wave after wave of pleasure wash over me and I am lost to it.

19 CLADE

DAISY

My eyes pop open and I freeze for a brief moment, unsure of my surroundings. I'm no longer in the medical unit with the other abductees. Images come together in my mind of our rescue. I let out a shaky breath, remembering how Darnok stormed into the room, covered in blood and gore, and how I didn't give a good goddamn. Warmth floods my chest as recall how he opened his arms when I flung myself at him. In that moment nothing mattered except that we were together again.

My mind skips over all the details and lingers over the lovemaking we shared last night. My gentle warrior worried over me and fought his instincts to maintain some semblance of control during our mating. I remember those big scarred hands gliding over my skin and his mouth provoking an orgasm so hard it made my entire body seize up. Everything about last night was amazing.

My hand goes to the heavy warmth draped over my waist. If I'd thought it was his arm, I'd have been very mistaken. It's his thick tail. The upper part is as thick as my arm, thus the misunderstanding. Reaching over, I drag my open palm down it until I find the end. He shifts slightly on the bed as I examine the tip of his tail. It has a round bulbous tip, almost like a barrel, the size of my fist. I run it over my lips, enjoying the slightly rough texture.

My new mate rumbles, "Do you wish more sex my queen? Handling a male's tail is an excellent way to make that fact known."

I look over my shoulder to see him gazing at me. "Tails are a secondary sex characteristic? I don't remember reading about that in the database."

He reaches for me, turning me to face him. "There is much to learn about me that you will not find in the database, my queen."

Smiling, I realize he's trying to flirt. How adorable. Scooting closer, I bring the tip of his tail to my mouth again. Looking him in the eyes, I lick over the end and blow on it. As I predicted, it makes him shiver. "You have a sexy tail, my takadon."

His eyes light up. Clearly the man is pleased to be sporting a brand-new title, one designating him as my one and only male.

His hand comes out to rest on my hip. It's warm and he caresses my skin with his thumb. "I cannot believe you selected me from all the males in the armada." Glancing down at the tip of his tail nestled between my hands, he swallows thickly and I see his wings jerk behind him. "I will do my very best to ensure you do not regret taking me to you."

I smile up at him. "There's no chance of that happening. I like everything about you."

He glances away and I remember he thought of himself as a failure because I got taken in battle. Reaching out, I tickle under his chin with his own tail. His eyes get big and I can't help but laugh. "Thank you for rescuing me, my takadon."

"Thank you for figuring out a way to contact us. The information you provided made it possible for us to locate you and the others. If not for that, we might still be searching for you."

He's still talking, saying something about how he doesn't want to give up command of our ship because he doesn't think anyone can keep me safe. I have to admit that it's going in one ear and out the other. I'm distracted by his earnest facial features and his smell. Oh my God, it's absolutely amazing. I interrupt him, blurting out the first words that come to mind. "You still smell fantastic. How much longer is that going to last?"

He stops talking, his mouth snapping shut in an instant. A slow sexy smile takes over his mouth. "I am pleased you enjoy my mating scent. It will remain overwhelming until I am carrying your young." He pauses, looking smug as hell. When I don't speak, he continues. "It might take being exposed to your pheromones several times in rapid succession to ignite parthenogenesis."

I vaguely remember that happens when they are exposed to a female's pheromones. An egg will be released into a small sac in the side of his stomach. When it grows to about the size of a thumbnail, it will be released and placed in an incubation chamber. I remember reading about the process. It was such a strange concept that I closed down the tutorial and took some time to let it sink in. It's why I have no idea how long it takes the eggs to mature or anything else about hatchlings.

Grinning, I realize that I'll have to get back to learning all about that. I make a mental note to do that right after I enjoy some more sex with my new alien husband. He's stopped talking and is staring at me, his eyes warm and accepting. I bring his tail to my lips, open my mouth, and wrap my lips around it. Then I make a production out of sucking it like I did his cock last night. Darnok is on me in an instant and I'm getting some major dick action, just like I wanted. For the very first time, my life is looking up and it's all thanks to this big sexy warrior.

I WAKE UP HOURS LATER, exhausted from hours upon hours of sex in every conceivable position. It was all amazing and something about Darnok's sperm is soothing, ensuring I never got chafed or sore. Draconians are an amazing species in more ways than one.

I'm disappointed to find his mating scent has dissipated somewhat. Then it hits me what that means. I scoot down the bed and examine the area on his hip where he carries eggs. Sure enough it's slightly warm to the touch and swelling a little.

Darnok stretches and makes a chuffing sound I think might be laughter. "You must be patient, my queen. Making young takes many cycles." I gently cover the area with my hand. His hand comes down to cover mine and I'm truly awestruck. Cognitively, I know that I might be pregnant from all the amazing sex, but knowing for certain he is carrying our young warms me from the inside out. I glance up to catch his eye before lifting our hands and placing a soft kiss over the growing bulge.

He places his hands under my arms and hauls me up until we are face-to-face. His expression is guarded and a little vulnerable. "You are truly pleased that I am with young?"

Nodding, I find myself tearing up a little. "I'm more than pleased with you, my takadon. For the first time in my life everything is perfect and you have made it so." Reaching out, I wrap my arms around his neck and snuggle up on his chest. One wing comes out to wrap around me, covering me from my shoulders to my ankles. I sigh contentedly. "Nothing feels better than being under your wing."

He tugs me closer, nuzzling my hair a bit before tucking my head securely under his chin. "I prefer keeping you close. You are too precious to me to ever again leave your safety to chance."

My stomach rumbles loudly and I cringe because I know he's going to jump to his feet to find food for me. When he moves, I go with him. He keys in a request for food into his handheld and then slings his legs over the side of the bed. I lie back against the bed with my arms over my head, enjoying the view of my new naked husband. He's an amazing specimen. Even compared to the other warriors, he's huge and has muscles sitting on top muscles.

Coming to my knees, I wrap my arms around one shoulder. Kissing a gigantic scar running from his neck to his elbow, I ask, "How did you get this one, handsome?"

He glances down at the scar and his face lights up with a smile. "Roan was almost trapped between a bulkhead and an emergency a piece of machinery that had broken off its housing unit during a battle when we were but younglings."

"You saved him and got injured in the process."

"I shoved him out of the way and took the full brunt of the injury myself."

I know I'm missing something, some small bit of information that will make Darnok's decision to take a proverbial bullet make sense. "Were you and Roan close?"

His wings lift and his horns come up in a gesture I interpret as pride. "My sire took Roan in when he was a hatchling. Roan was a breeder, raised among warriors. To say he was revered by my family would be an understatement."

I nod, not really understanding what he's trying to communicate. Darnok adds helpfully, "Roan was destined to breed for a queen, while we were destined to die for one." Slapping his chest, his chin comes up in a gesture that's dominant. "He lived to bring hatchlings into the world, because I acted quickly and prioritized his safety over my own."

My mouth falls open. I finally get it. It's all about continuing their lines. Breeders are important because they are the ones tasked with making babies. My hand drops down to the egg sack gently pulsating on his hip. "Correct me if I'm wrong, but you are bringing hatchlings into the world for a queen as well."

His face lights up with a smile so bright it could challenge the sun. I cup his face in my hands and try to communicate what's on my mind in a respectful way. "From now on, I want you to understand your own worth. You protected a queen and are carrying her hatchlings. From this point forward, I want you to prioritize yourself in exactly the same manner you did your friend."

It takes a minute for the shock to wear off his face. Then he swallows thickly and nods. "You are correct, my queen. I will not risk myself while carrying for you."

Shaking my head, I try again. "You will not risk yourself if it can be avoided, whether you are carrying or not. Because you are my one and only male, the safety of our entire line rests with you. If you allow yourself to be injured or killed, think of all the young waiting to be hatched that will never see the light of day."

His hands come out hard and fast around my shoulders

and understanding lights his face. "I am intent upon remaining in control of our vessel. We will lead and craft battle plans to protect all, but I will not leave your side again."

"I like that compromise. You still get to be the warrior you always were and I don't have to see you risking yourself on the front lines of every battle."

"I will still fight if it becomes necessary to protect you or our young."

"Don't think for a minute that I won't fight to protect our little ones. I might lose but I'll go down fighting."

His mouth drops open, much as mine did before. "As you wish, my queen."

The door chimes. Darnok moves quickly, grabbing his uniform. He shoves his feet down each leg and slides it on halfway, with the top part hanging off his waist. I scramble to pull up some of the thin blanket to cover myself. Watching him stroll to the door makes me smile. Every inch of that amazing man belongs to me.

He steps back and Roan steps into the doorway, holding a box of food. His nose wrinkles. "You need to shower and air out this room. Your mating scent is revolting."

Darnok shrugs. "It is nowhere near as horrendous as yours was when you mated the Draconian queen." Somehow I can tell by the tone of his voice that my sweet warrior is proud of how awful his friend finds his mating scent.

Roan is still standing in front of the door, like he's planning to make a run for it at any second. Even I'm amused at this point.

His voice turns serious. "I have brought you a mating present, Darnok."

My mate's eyes drop to the box of food his friend is

carrying. "I am grateful for your gift. My queen is much in need of sustenance."

Roan tenses and then states quietly, "Remain calm, my friend." When he steps away from the door, another male is standing outside. His eyes jump from Darnok to me and back again, as if he's terrified of being caught looking at a newly mated female.

Darnok's wings unfurl and he takes a step forward. His shocked voice sounds unsteady. "Kane, you are among the warriors in our armada? I did not think to search the database for..." His mouth snaps shut and he gestures toward the seating area. "I forget myself. Come in, brother. You are forever welcome in our space."

As the man makes his way forward, I climb out of bed. Careful to wrap myself up in the blanket for modesty, I move over to stand near Darnok. Kane's eyes slide over to me again and my anxious warrior does the last thing I expect. He steps in front of me, blocking his brother's view. I immediately begin to question if this is his real brother or if their relationship is a brothers-in-arms type of thing. Kane's shadow moves backward toward the door.

Roan's voice sounds off from nearby. "You are newly chosen, Darnok. Control your instincts. Your brother does not wish to take your queen."

Darnok literally growls, clearly angry. "This I know, Roan." There is a short silence and he makes another exasperated sound and I realize Darnok can't come up with a good explanation for his overprotective behavior.

Kane finally speaks. "You have my respect for earning the notice of a queen, brother. Roan is correct about your mating scent. I've never smelled anything so revolting in my entire life." He reaches something out to Darnok and takes a respectful step back. I don't know what's in the package, but whatever it is clicks down Darnok's anxiety level.

Darnok's shoulders relax a bit. He folds his wings neatly behind his back again and seems more composed. "Thank you, brother. I am pleased you are here, but..."

The other man interrupts. "But you need a moment to eat, cleanse yourself, and ground yourself in your female's scent before meeting with me. I understand how unsettling this must be for you. None of us ever expected to have a queen or young."

I know better than to speak up while standing here wearing nothing but a flimsy bed covering. It wouldn't take much to set my overprotective warrior off again, so I let them iron out their temporary goodbyes. Roan shoves the box of food into Darnok's hands at some point and he's juggling the food and the gift from his brother.

When they are out the door, he turns to me looking embarrassed. "Forgive the intrusion, my queen."

I can't keep the smile off my face. "Your brother could never be considered an intrusion. I'm really excited to discover that we have an actual blood relative among the warriors."

He gestures over to a small table and when I slide into the seat, he begins unpacking food for us. Of course I am so ecstatic that I can't keep my mouth shut for anything. "You have a brother here! We should invite him over for dinner. Do you have any idea what he does for a living?"

Darnok brings up a bite of food to my lips, smiling indulgently. "He's a warrior, my queen. All the males of my line are but simple warriors."

I take the bit he offers, chewing quickly. "All except you, right? You're a hero, a takadon, and soon to be a sire."

He takes a bite himself, appearing happier than I can

ever remember him being. "What you say is true. I have been blessed by the goddess. My sire would be proud."

"Heck, anyone would be proud to have a son like you. Your brother is proud of you. I could tell by the tone of his voice. He looks a lot like you."

"Warriors from the same sire bear a striking resemblance to one another. It is the way with our kind."

"Like you, he's drop-dead gorgeous. We should help him find a wife."

"I think we should not interfere with his mating." There is a gentle chiding to his voice. My handsome husband is using a chiding voice with a queen. Will wonders never cease? I sputter, "It's not interfering. Really, it's not."

He simply feeds me more small bites of food as I gush about how great it's going to be for our kids to have a real live blood relative around. I mention how Kane can help them learn to fly and important stuff like that. Darnok loses it.

I gaze into his laughing face and he finally gets ahold of himself enough to explain. "Draconian hatchlings fly of their own accord before they can speak, crawl, or even understand words. We're forced to leash them to heavy objects or they would wander off and get lost. Trust me, no one needs to teach a hatchling to fly, my queen."

I full-on grin. "Then he can help us keep up with all of them. You're going to have three or four and I'll have at least one. Twins run in my family, so I might give birth to two at the same time. It's not unheard of for human women to have triplets even."

That wipes the smile right off his face. "Between the two of us, we could end up with as many as breeders spawn."

I nod. "Anything's possible, handsome."

He's quiet while we finish our meal. Then he leads me to the cleansing unit.

"What are you thinking so hard about, my takadon?"

His head comes up and his expression is so serious it makes me wonder if he regrets agreeing to be my mate. "We can no longer afford to drift in the slipstream of the other queens. Right now you are forced to share a ship with Meiko and Aiko. You deserve your own vessel."

I relax a little, relieved that he's just worried about status. "I don't value being the only queen onboard a ship. Human women like to share…"

"I cannot keep you safe if two other queens constantly feel the need to assert their authority. Even when I was making plans to rescue you, one of the queens proved to be a distraction by insisting upon coming with me. We argued and I sent her from the bridge."

"I can't believe one of them did that." Then again, I can believe it.

"We need our own ship, one that only we control. Our young will need every advantage we can give them if they are to survive and thrive in this new sector of space we're to inhabit. I will not allow my young to see you constantly vying for power with the other queens."

I guess we've bumped into some kind of Draconian custom that I don't know about. I nod, "Whatever you say, my takadon."

His wings relax and his horns slip back a bit. "We also need to establish a family stronghold once we find a planet to colonize."

I suddenly feel like a feckless fool next to this serious warrior. He's talking about building a dynasty, protecting our children, and ensuring they grow up healthy and happy. Me, on the other hand, I'm just thinking about hanging around my two friends and drifting along. I sober up, suddenly aware of how perilous the 'verse can be. "When it comes to safety, I trust your judgment. If you feel strongly about us having a stronghold or a ship of our own, I'll do whatever is necessary to help you make that happen."

His arms come out around me. "You will follow my lead?"

Nodding, I run my soapy hands over his chest. "Of course I'll follow your lead. You're the warrior and are vested with the responsibility of protecting our family."

"I *am* your warrior and it is an honor to serve you, my queen."

I grin. "Being a warrior, you've probably forgotten more about keeping us safe that I'll ever know."

"I will teach you to be more safety conscious, but you must leave the fighting to my clade."

The translation programming is substituting the word clan for clade. Warmth spreads through my chest. We do have a clan now that his brother showed up. "Let's hurry. I want to meet your brother and get to work looking for a new ship."

"The Moltan vessel escaped but I saw several mid-bulk trade vessels on the tarmac when we landed."

Shoving off his chest, I rinse off and jump out of the cleansing unit. "Let's go call dibs on the best one."

He pulls me back in and hits the drying cycle. I always forget about the drying. Since there aren't any towels, the drying cycle is kind of critical. When we leave the cleansing unit, I begin looking for my clothing. I quickly discover it lying on the floor, torn up too badly to wear. I pick it up and shove it in a reclamation slot.

Darnok begins tearing the covering off the package his brother brought. Inside is a beautiful set of uniforms.

They're black with bright blue piping. Mine fits perfectly. "How long were we locked in this shuttle that your brother had time to custom make uniforms for us?"

"We've been here two cycles. The bots can make a new uniform in a few microns with the right programming."

Shock makes my hands still at my throat. After a second, I continue adjusting the collar. "It doesn't feel like we've been here for two days." I vaguely remember Darnok feeding me nutrition bars and pressing a hydration packet in my hand multiple times.

"Did you even eat over the last couple of days?"

He turns away. "I did not know how long our mating cycle would last. I did not wish to waste food on myself if it meant dealing with males bringing food."

Reaching out to grasp his shoulder, I gasp. "What?"

Turning back to look at me, his lips press into a firm line. "I did not trust myself not to attack them, especially if they dared to cast their eyes upon you during your heat."

I take another leap forward in understanding Draconian males. The more primitive part of their brain must assert itself during mating. Realization dawns that when he says during my heat, he means when I'm ovulating. It makes a certain kind of sense. He'll deny himself food rather than risk another male being around me when I'm in heat. I file that handy bit of information away for future reference.

20 SETTLEMENT

DARNOK

When we leave the shuttle, I am better able to cope with other males gazing at my new queen. She looks lovely with her long flowing hair, bright blue eyes, and form-fitting uniform. My female glides along, totally unaware that most every warrior is sneaking glances at her. They see the unity emblem on our uniforms and are likely wondering what possessed her to choose me as her takadon. I know they were reluctant to approach her once word got out that I was serving as her protector. The other warriors fear me for my fighting prowess. I can be vicious when the need arises, so I do not blame them. I recognized myself in the database of human culture and customs. I am what they would call a berserker in battle.

Warriors are taught from an early age to function in a group. We are groomed to value unity and common purpose. Their primary reaction being fear has only ever caused problems before now.

For the first time in my life, being feared by lesser warriors has worked in my favor. It kept them from approaching my beautiful queen while I got my head together and will keep them all at arm's distance now that we are mated. They aren't wrong to be cautious of me, especially when it comes to my queen.

Roan and Kane move to greet us and I'm surprised that I feel no animosity toward them. Now that I am thinking more clearly, it is a wonder that I ever felt that way about my best friend and my own brother.

I step forward to meet them halfway, with my queen at my back. "Greetings, brethren."

Kane's face lights up. It's good to see the cautiousness replaced by cheerfulness. His deep voice is the note of familiarity that I have been missing in my life. "Greetings, my brother. And congratulations on being chosen by a queen." Dropping to one knee before my queen, he bows his head. "Greetings, Queen Daisy. I welcome you to our clade."

I am choked with emotion that my brother welcomes her to our family like the queens of old. This is the deepest respect a male can show for another's queen and I am grateful for his consideration. My queen seems more confused than impressed.

She stumbles over her words. "Thank you, Kane... for the gracious welcome. Please stand and come talk with us."

Kane rises and approaches with a smile that gladdens my heart. We touch each other's shoulders the way warriors are wont to do. I motion for Roan to join us. "Where is the lovely Queen Meiko today, Roan?"

"She has forsaken me. Come sit in the shade. Much has happened over the two cycles you were swamped in your mating lust."

I laugh at his turn of phrase because he is not far off the mark. We follow him over to a spot where several trees meet. The sky is pink, as is the sun, and most of the strange vegetation is purple and red. The planet is lush and I can scent the salty ocean in the air.

Pulling my queen down into my lap, I ask curiously, "What have we missed?"

Kane drops a handful of tiny geodes into my queen's lap. Each has been sawed in half. The gemstones are brilliant and each contains a different color.

My queen sits up, clearly impressed with the jewels. "Wow, this is quite a collection, Kane." Holding one up in the air, she twirls it around for us to see. It is impressive, particularly in her small hands, for it looks larger than it is.

Kane drops down onto the ground beside us. "It is my mating gift to you, Queen Daisy."

"I couldn't accept such a generous gift. These must be worth a fortune."

Kane shoots me an exasperated look. I speak up immediately. "You will accept them, my sweet queen, and they will become the first heirlooms of our line."

Glancing between me and Kane, she finally acquiesces to our demand that she accept them. "When you put it that way, I can hardly refuse. Thank you, Kane. I'll keep them safe and ensure they are passed down to all the young of our clade."

"You honor me, Queen Daisy. My brother was fortunate to have been chosen by such a sweet and unselfish queen."

I'm pleased that they are getting along so well. "Where did these gemstones come from?"

"This planet is rich with gemstones and minerals. They are not only plentiful but close to the surface. Roan and I have been gathering them since we arrived."

"I see the wisdom of gathering such a valuable resource.

We have a queen to look after and it's likely both of you will end up with queens as well."

Roan chimes in. "That is the least of our news, Darnok. Queen Cassandra has laid claim to this pristine new world. We are to settle here permanently."

"She claimed it by right of conquest?"

"Not exactly. The remaining Sparloc were turned over to those who enforce the law in this sector of space. They have been charged with trafficking in queens. Since there were none left to object, she laid claim to this world. The council of elders in this region have allowed her to keep all the possessions belonging to our enemies in recompense for the loss of life we sustained rescuing the queens."

"That's bullshit. It's not like we can replace the lives of fallen warriors with things of monetary value."

All three sets of eyes turn on my enraged queen. My brother speaks before I can gesture for him to remain silent. "Warriors are born to die for their queens. Our fallen warriors would wish our queens to be compensated for their sacrifice."

Turning on my lap to face him, her angry voice only gets angrier. "I've got a better idea. Why don't we stop acting like warriors are expendable? Now that we have our own home world, we need to set up planetary defenses and come up with a plan to keep everyone safe, not just women."

I can see Kane's face struggle to remain impassive as he tries to work out if my queen is speaking in earnest. I save him the trouble. "My queen sees warriors and queens as equal. She values our lives in ways we do not."

Kane's eyes catch mine for a brief second before looking away. "Would that our own queens had been so generous. Our family might still be together."

I open my mouth to speak but no words come out.

A short silence spins out between the four of us before Kane speaks again. "Roan assisted me in laying claim to one of the buildings for our clade. Very few queens have formalized their mating. The few that did were given buildings to ensure their privacy, while we work on erecting a city worthy of housing them."

I speak up again. "My queen and I believe it would be best if our clade had a ship. We don't need anything elaborate, just something to evacuate our clade if we are attacked."

Kane nods. "That was my thought as well. Once I learned that you were chosen, I did all within my power to establish a strong position for us on this world. Roan is known to Queen Cassandra and was able to negotiate us a ship."

I glance at Roan and he nods. "I had to agree that our clade would complete one hundred trade runs over the next five thousand cycles."

"Roan and I can see to that while you breed for your queen. The ship is nothing to brag about, but with the gemstones we've gathered, it's reasonable to expect that we can have it retrofitted into something worthy of safeguarding your queen should the need arise. We are permitted to retain the shuttle your queen used for her first breeding."

I notice that my queen is just trying to take in all the information we are discussing. I'm curious about our new world. "Have you had time to survey the planet?"

"No, we've spent our time gathering resources and working on the ship."

"Might I suggest we use the shuttle to survey the planet for ourselves? We could do a more thorough scan for resources, see if there are herd beasts that might serve as a food source and decompress from the stress of trying to get established."

Both Roan and Kane seem interested, but Roan quips, "After you perform an air purification cycle. I honestly can't stand the smell."

Daisy laughs. Rather than talking about my mating scent, she addresses Roan. "What of your young?"

"They are well cared for in the hatchery, Queen Daisy. You have no need to worry over them."

"Don't you think they might enjoy getting some fresh air?"

His gaze turns assessing. "You care about my young?"

"You're a member of our clade, so it's natural that care I about them." Her face falls and she stammers, "If you don't feel comfortable having them around me, that's fine. I know we don't know each other very well."

"I thought I knew Meiko well but apparently I didn't." After a thoughtful moment, his face brightens. "If you truly do not mind having them around, I will bring them."

She claps with happiness before she thinks about it. It's a childish but cute gesture. Even Kane laughs along with her.

Daisy

Sitting in the front of the shuttle, I lean forward to get a better view out the window that's really just an electronic viewing screen designed to look like a window. It strikes me as funny that someone thought to do that. The majestic beauty of the scenery we're flying over takes my breath away. I can't wait to get out and see more of it up close.

Two of Roan's little ones are toddler-sized and are being

allowed to simply sit on the console and gaze at the screen. It doesn't seem safe to me, but I'm not their father. They're really adorable plump little beings with fat bellies and frail wings. Their horns are more like nubs. I can't help but smile at the way they keep putting their heads together to whisper before looking over their shoulder at me. They must think I'm the smallest and weirdest queen they've ever seen, assuming of course they've ever seen a woman at all. They have cute high-pitched laughs and their wings shake when they giggle.

Darnok's voice whispers in my ear. "You like hatchlings, do you not?"

Looking up at the little ones kicking at each other's feet on the console, I realize that I can't wait until I can hold my own hatchlings.

"They're cute little mischievous cherubs. What's not to like."

I wait patiently while his translator cues him on what cherubs are and then he smiles. "I see the resemblance, my queen."

I swallow hard and tears sting my eyes. I see alarm jump onto Darnok's face but I hold up one hand. "I just can't believe after everything we've been through we're finally here and safe."

"The planets in this sector have an accord. They have agreed to keep an eye out for the Moltan vessel. I suspect they are many parsecs from this world. You are safe, my queen. Rest easy and enjoy our day in the sunshine."

Nodding, I blink back my tears. It's hard shifting gears. Memories pop into my head unbidden, reminding me of the abuse we suffered at the hands of the aquatics and the threat of being changed into something not human by the Moltan. It sometimes feels like I'm two different people, the woman who was locked away and the one who is virtually worshiped by her mate. I desperately want to be something in between, a real live flesh and blood woman willing to step out of this shuttle and make a better life for myself and these males.

The shuttle lands on a ridgeline and we all exit the shuttle. Kane and Roan have leashed his little ones but I gotta give them credit, they're doing their very best to break free. One is standing on his leash, yanking the other side with all his might. He's muttering something and two are more bent down, giving him hand signals. Sometimes hatchlings don't seem like toddlers at all.

Darnok leads me out to stand on a precipice. He wraps one wing around me to shield me from the wind. That's totally unnecessary as the weather is really nice, but I don't object, because I like snuggling close to him. We look out over a vast pink ocean and he points to something in the valley below. "It looks like a herd of some kind. I wonder what they are."

"I don't know, but we'll find out if they're fit for the belly of queen this day."

"I don't think Kane and Roan are going to get the little ones to calm down long enough to hunt."

Reaching out, I touch Darnok's side. His egg pouch is still relatively flat but it's warm and pulsating. I love touching him there and am being extremely careful not to be too rough. "I don't want you out there hunting while you're in such a delicate state."

His head snaps down to stare at me, clearly baffled and a little offended. "I am not weak, my queen."

I jump onto my toes to give him a kiss on the lips. "I know you aren't weak. That's the kind of thing women got told back on Earth when they were pregnant."

"Ah, you jest with me." His gaze turns adoring. "I like that." Darnok's hand covers mine and he tells me something I don't know. "The scan tells me there are two."

Flinging my arms around his neck, I drag him back down and kiss him until I can't breathe. "We're having twins?"

"Breeders have more, but two is the limit of what I will carry for you, my queen."

"Two is fantastic. You won't ever find me complaining about how many hatchlings you carry for us. We need to create a hatchery, right?"

Nodding, he cups the side of my face with one scarred hand. "I will make sure one is constructed on our ship and in our temporary home."

"We're really doing this, aren't we? Making a family together and living our happily ever after?"

"Yes we are, my queen. I dare anyone to stand in the way of your happiness."

"You mean *our* happiness, right?"

Grinning, he nods and tucks the back of my head under his chin. It's an awkward pose because he is so much larger than me, but it allows us both to admire the amazing landscape. "I have a good gut feeling about this planet, Darnok."

My big warrior agrees. "Queen Cassandra means to raise a large modern city near our settlement. Roan says she's intent on luring human queens from Earth for all the warriors and has asked the surrounding planets to sign trade agreements with us."

I tilt my head so I can gaze up at him. "Cassandra and Mathadar are good negotiators. With any luck this might turn out to be the best move we've made thus far."

His voice cracks with emotion. "I am still stunned that we are welcomed with open arms. In our sector of space we are tasked with enforcing the will of the Draconian Queens. That makes us both feared and despised by the beings of that sector."

"That was your old life, my takadon. Things are different now. Instead of destroying worlds and doing the bidding of queens infected with evil parasites, you've just got me to worry about."

His lips descend to drop a kiss onto my forehead. "You are the being I wish to spend all my time pleasing."

"That's real sweet. I want to spend the rest of my life making you happy as well."

Turning slightly in his arms, our lips meet for the longest and sweetest kiss we've ever shared. Just when I settle down for some major league lip-locking, cute little sighing noises accompanied with small gusts of wind interrupt our moment.

When I turn around, I'm not all that surprised to find two of Roan's little ones fluttering nearby. They dip in the air and giggle, making little kissing noises before flying away. Roan snags each of them by one foot and gives us an apologetic shrug. I can't help but laugh and my uptight scarred warrior joins me.

EPILOGUE

TWO YEARS LATER

Darnok

My once-sweet queen has turned fierce. She stalks through the new vessel, inspecting every detail. She looks under bulkheads, inside consoles, and even peers into all the special access areas to make sure they lead where they are supposed to lead. To think that at one time she didn't think she had it in her to be a queen is difficult to fathom.

Now that we have young to safeguard, she refuses to tolerate anything but the best for them. I am used to Draconian queens, who not only care little for their own young but have a tendency to reap them repeatedly. This is the reason I once avoided queens at all costs.

My Daisy is nothing less than dedicated to me and our nine young hatchlings. Though we have elder caregivers, she feeds them, bathes them, plays with them, and takes turns taking them out with us. Today, she has our youngest tucked under her arm as she moves through the ship. He's only three weeks hatched, and just out of the incubator.

He looks just like me without all the scars, and my mate

adores him. A soft sock falls off his little foot. I pick it up and quickly slip it back into place. He rolls over in her arms and reaches for me. She reluctantly hands him over and I am thrilled to have him on my shoulder. He cuddles around my shoulder muscle and digs his toes into me. This is something they do to me but not their mother. It's like they instinctively know I have hard plating on my skin and she does not.

Our little ones are clever. I argue that they got their intelligence from me, since they are genetically all Draconian. My Daisy believe it is because she nurtures them and plays games with them that strengthen their minds, that they are smart. Truth be told, I think it is both, but I will not say such. A male has to hang on to his dignity after all.

I wait patiently as she bargains down the seller to something I consider absurd. He agrees to her price, likely because this is our seventh visit and he tires of dealing with her many peculiarities. This human mate of mine is sweet, loving, and kind beyond words. She is also deadly serious when it comes to ensuring the future of our clade.

Kane and Roan have long since found human brides, but my Daisy is more the queen mother of our clade than the others. They go to her for advice and we all listen to her wisdom.

When the deal is struck and the sales contract registered, we sit in on the bridge and enjoy the ambiance of our new home.

"Can you believe we traded in our sprawling compound for a starship?"

The question may sound like she has regrets, but I know better. "This is the safest ship made in this sector. I'd say if we were going to trade in a life of leisure, this would be the vessel worth trading it to obtain."

Reaching out, she runs her hand down our little one's back, stopping to play with his wings. He's sleeping and barely moves. "That's why I kept coming back to this ship. It's got the space we're looking for and it's fast and well armed."

"You do love being on a ship, my Daisy."

She grins. "I didn't think you were ever going to stop calling me your queen."

"Don't worry, I still think of you as my queen." Glancing around I have to admit she made a good choice. "This is a ship fit for a queen and safe enough for our spawn."

She nods, releasing a quick breath. "It's only temporary. When we've gotten all your brothers in this sector, we'll settle down for good planet side."

"You are a queen, so what you say must be true," I tease her gently. "However, I can't imagine you ever giving up your love of roaming the stars."

She watches me put our little one in his self-contained sleeping unit. I close the door, careful to lock it securely or he'll wake and wander off. "There's always something new and interesting to be seen in the 'verse. Some new person to meet, new trade deal to make, or new food to sample. It's exciting to do something different every day."

"We risk a lot in seeking a way to communicate with Draconian space."

"When we first left, we thought all the males knew about the symbionts. In the last two years others have escaped with stories of how the symbionts killed off all those with the knowledge of their control of that region of space. Finding a way to communicate is the only way we can ensure they have a fighting chance at overthrowing the symbionts. I won't leave an entire sector of space at their mercy."

Slipping a wing around my mate, I understand compassion is her dominant personality characteristic. "I am proud to be your mate. Others escape the rule of Draconian queens and wish nothing more than to put the memory behind them. You are one of a small number of queens intent upon seeking freedom for my kind."

"Liberating Exion space and recovering the remainder of your family is worth risking everything for, Darnok."

"We are lucky to have a means to skirt around Exion space, looking for a way across the barrier that divides it from the Naxis."

"There has to be a way and I don't care how long it takes, I'm going to find it."

I cover her dainty hand with my large scarred one and look her in the eyes. "I vowed to follow you until the end of time and I stand by that promise. Where you go, I follow."

Her eyes drift over my body and I can tell she loves what she sees. "I believe I mentioned something about rewarding you for your dedication, did I not?

"You know all about the rewards I like best, my queen."

"This ship belongs to us now."

"I well know how you enjoy sexing in every new space we own. I see no reason for this vessel to be any different. However, I believe it is my turn to do the rewarding."

Standing, she takes my hand and leads me away. I grab our little one's hovering habitat and turn on the stasis feature. Better that he does not see or hear things he cannot yet understand. Our newly hatched spend most of their time sleeping, so I do not think he will wake in any event.

Setting him safely aside when we enter the master suite, I allow my sweet queen to lead me to the sleeping platform.

I stand in the middle of the floor and she steps around me. "You smell amazing."

"It is your imagination. I am not of a state to carry young again quite yet."

She replies, happily, "I never said you were, my sweet. Though your mating scent is intoxicating, I actually think you smell nice all the time."

"That can't be right. Warriors are hardworking and smelly."

"How about we just go for hard?"

"I've been there for most of the morning, my Daisy."

"Seeing me negotiating a trade gives you a hard-on? How did I never know that?"

"You clearly haven't been paying attention as of late."

Her hands come out to tug at the seam of my uniform. "We both know that's not true." Cool air hits my chest when she pull it back off my shoulders. My queen loves to undress me and I adore having her hands on me.

"I am lucky to enjoy your attention frequently. Some of the other mated warriors are not so fortunate."

"Let's not get off track talking about other men. You're the only man I want to discuss." Her hands smooth down my hips and she slowly lowers the dark cloth, shoving it down my legs. "Have you truly been feeling neglected?"

Taking one of her hands, I wrap it around my cock. "I could lie and say yes so you can make me up." I hear the hopefulness in my own voice and it almost makes me laugh.

She goes to her knees and I hear her chuckle. "The term is make it up to you, not make you up."

"Humans have many strange turns of phrase. It is diffi-cult to remember them all."

"How about we play a new game? Every time you get a really obscure saying right, I'll give you a treat." She warms my cock with her breath before licking around the tip.

"What warrior could resist such a tempting offer?"

Looking up at me, she teases, "I've yet to hear an obscure human saying from you this morning."

I rack my brain trying to come up with something I've heard human females say. My Daisy blows across my damp skin again, making me groan. An idea flies into my head and comes right out of my mouth before I can think better of it. "Are you going to shoot the breeze this day or suck my cock?" I still, waiting to see if I got the human expression right.

She doesn't say anything but her mouth closes over my cock and she sucks until her cheeks sink inward. It feels just as amazing as it did the very first time she pleasured me. I crave her mouth, enjoy gazing into her beautiful blue eyes, and can't resist tangling my hand in her long pale strands. Like always, I'm overly eager and rock my hips slightly.

Among my people it was considered foolish to have sex without intent to make young. Queens did not breed for pleasure, only for procreation. Human queens are much different. Their delicate bodies burst with need, and sex for pure pleasure is expected. Closing my eyes, I just enjoy her mouth on my heated flesh.

Sucking me turns her on. I can always tell because the air fills with the scent of her arousal. It makes my mouth water and my mind remember how delicious my female tastes. Unable to drive the idea of tasting her out of my mind, I pull her to her feet.

My claws rip at her uniform and I unintentionally tear it trying to remove it. This is not a new problem and the reason she travels with an extra set of clothing in the compartment below our hatchling's sleeping unit. Within moments she is naked.

Every single time I see her markings of motherhood my heart squeezes in my chest. I kneel and run my fingers over the scars. When I first mated her, there was not one blemish on her pale skin. She bore me a Draconian son and this is the evidence of her dedication. Our young are large and my queen is small. Leaning over, I rain handfuls of human kesses over her stomach.

"Your marks make you even more beautiful in my eyes."

"Keep talking sweetheart and you're never going to get rid of me."

I love when she makes the jest with me. She well knows I will never tolerate being separated from her. "I wish that I had a scar to remind me of our love."

"If you don't get to work pleasuring your mate, that can be arranged."

She's smiling and her voice is teasing, so I decide to make up my own game. Running my fingers gently over her mound, I glance up at her. "Now that I have played your mating game, you must play mine."

"Tell me, my takadon."

"You must tell me what I would do if I were king for a day. You will be rewarded only for correct answers."

"Oh I see, it's a game to find out how well I know my takadon."

I blow over her tender flesh, much as she did mine earlier. My cock is the hardest it's ever been, bobbing between my legs. I ignore it in favor of playing sex games with my lovely mate.

"You're a real tease. Let's see, you'd start with morning sex since you conveniently wake up with a hard-on every day."

"Correct." I drape one of her legs over my shoulder and give her a nice long lick along the seam of her pussy.

She quickly thinks up something else to prove how well she knows her mate. "You would forbid everyone from having doma because you hate the crumbs getting everywhere."

I give my clever queen what she wants and she scrambles to come up with ever more absurd demands I would make if I ruled our world. She mentions that I would have her wear a cloaking device so no other males could look at her, which does not sound like a bad idea to my ears She thinks that I would decree there to be only one meal. It would be at midday and involve only morning food. Again she is correct. Before the humans came to us, there was only food. Now there is morning and night food, sweet food and food we only eat on certain holidays. I shake with laughter when she points out that all the small furry pets the queens laid claim to would be rounded up and placed in a huge match where there would be only one surviving victor and it would be shared equally between all the queens to cut down on the noise. She goes on and on with ever more ridiculous scenarios. I wish I could say they were all lies but alas they all have a grain of truth to them.

When her legs are quivering and she is mad with need I stop, because I am evil that way. She reaches for my horns, but I stay her hands. My clever queen knows all too well that when I am aroused stroking my horns will make me wild enough with need to give her anything she wants. To be quite honest, it is how we got our third child. Anyway, I come to my feet and wrap my arms around her. I'm gratified when she melts into my touch.

"Every time is as exciting as the very first time with you, my takadon."

Running my finger around her pouting lips, I smile at her second attempt to get her way with me. "Horn stroking and sweet compliments will only get you so far with me, my sweet female. You know what it is I want from you."

She flings herself backward onto the bed and scoots back. I stand with my hands on my hips waiting for her to show me everything the gods have given her. She still turns pink from her generously sized breasts all the way up to her hairline as she spreads her long legs for me. Seeing her all laid out and ready for my cock creates the pinnacle of arousal for me each and every time.

"Don't make me beg, baby."

Ah, she uses her love name for me. I am sometimes called baby and at other times babe or handsome. Whatever name she calls me by when we are intimate it is always sweet and complimentary, but it's the tone of her voice that goes straight to my cock. Taking a step closer, I draw the moment out. "You wish me to cover you in my scent?"

"Yes, your scent, your sweat, and your seed."

I feel my resolve to draw out our pleasure slowly fracturing. She knows me too well and is saying all the things that arouse me the most. Climbing onto the bed, I skate the tips of my fingers over her soft skin. She's my idea of total luxury. "No male was ever as fortunate as me to have a queen such as you."

When she holds out her arms, my resolve crumbles and I go to her. Her lips find mine and the feelings between us heat up once more. I can't get enough of her lips, her scent, and her heat. My fingers slide through her folds, even as my mouth moves down to enjoy the tips of her breasts. "I miss the taste of your milk." Heated words are spoken without thought or agenda but she rewards me anyhow by raking her nails down my back and over my shoulders.

The scent of her arousal doubles and then triples and I revel in knowing I can make her so wet for me that she is out of her mind with need. It's proof that she feels the same about me that I do about her.

My greedy mouth licks, nips, and sucks her tender skin, and when I finally reach her sex, she opens wider for me. Latching on to the bundle of nerves, I suck and rub my tongue over it. When she comes screaming my name, I move up and position myself correctly to enter her body.

As always, she pulls me forward with her legs, impaling herself on my thick cock. This ritual of me looming large over her and her dragging me forward with her legs is getting to be a time-honored tradition between the two of us. I love that she takes what she wants from me. It makes me feel wanted and needed. I have told her more than once that heavy emotions come along with this cock of mine. She agrees. Our bond is stronger than most couples, I think.

But once I am fully seated inside her fair form, I can't think of anything but taking her hard and rough like we both like. There is a constant stream of dialogue from my pretty queen. She tells me everything that she would normally keep to herself. Things such as my cock is magnificent and we should think up a fitting name for him. I want to laugh at her naughty words but my cock is too hard for me to do anything but fuck.

When it comes to lovemaking, I am forever at her mercy it seems. I like giving pleasure as much as experiencing it and my queen is no novice at ensuring I get all the pleasure I deserve from our lovemaking. This day the bed shakes with the power of our joining, yet it is not enough.

I spread my wings and her eyes fly open wide. I remember all the times she's called me her dark angel. Images come forth in my mind of beings with dark wings made of feathers. Though I don't resemble these beautiful creatures at all, it's nice that my mate sees me as similar. I lift her with my arms until I am sitting on my knees and she is perched on my cock. I need her face-to-face with me, but she gets her feet under her and lifts off me. I know what's coming and ready myself.

Once she is on all fours, she pulls her hair to the side and looks back at me over her shoulder. This is it, my time to dominate her the way I most prefer. Placing my massive hand down between her shoulder blades, I press her down. She goes quietly, submitting to my wishes. When only her pretty ass is in the air, I move forward, covering her smaller form with my bulk. I say the dirtiest, filthiest thing I can think of. "Females are meant to submit to their male's cock." It's the opposite of everything I have been taught and it makes my queen shiver beneath me.

"You're in a naughty mood today, my king."

"Show this king how much you respect his cock by fucking yourself on it."

I'm uncertain where the words are coming from, but they have the desired effect. My sweet queen reaches back and positions my stiff cock and rises to press herself back, forcing it into her body. Her form shakes from the effort of taking me and it thrills me in a way I never thought possible.

This moment makes my life worth living. It's worth dying for as well. My queen submitting to my sexual needs amazes me and feeds the deepest darkest part of my soul. When she begins to lose her rhythm, I take over by placing one hand over her shoulder and pulling her roughly back. Sparks fly and she begins a steady stream of pleading.

I move faster and add more force until I'm moving her up the sleeping platform slightly. I add my tail to the mix and it pokes her tight rosette. That's all it takes for her to come apart beneath me. When her body locks down around my cock, I begin to spill my seed. We both seem to come forever until she is a sweaty compliant mess. I pull out and curl around her, stroking her soft skin and whispering sweet words to her.

I could easily go again, but my queen will need a bit to recover. This is the way with our lovemaking and I'd not have it any other way. Lying happy and sated with my beautiful queen in my arms, I marvel at how different my life is now. Before there were nightmares and hopelessness in the face of a Draconian queen. Now there is only respect, pleasure, and endless amounts of love flowing between us.

In this relationship there is also hope for the continuation of my line. I reach over and check on my little one. He is on one side, clutching one of the tiny stuffed creatures I made for my queen some years ago. Each of our young was encouraged to select one of them and they are now treasured possessions for our young.

Looking back I hardly recognize that anxious warrior who was so worried about caring for the queen he had no hope of being chosen by. Now I am content, sure of myself, and I have a clade once more. It's the difference between having a future to look forward to and having nothing. All thanks to my queen being able to see past the horrible scars to the warrior inside.

I snuggle closer to my sleeping queen. With our own ship under us, we have many options. I know not if finding my brothers is something we can manage, but I would give much to see them safely away from the cruel rule of Draconian queens. Before there was no hope of being reunited. Then Kane was discovered among the crew of our armada and I can't help but dream of seeing the others.

My father once said that a warrior's true worth was in

his heart and soul, not in his ability to kill in the name of his queen. For the longest time, I didn't understand the lesson he was trying to teach. Now I think his message was love and honor are more powerful than battle and killing. I wish he were here to see me now and meet his grandspawn.

Reaching out, I remove a strand of hair from my queen's face. She's so lovely lying cuddled to my side. Instinctively I cover her with my wing. The movement makes her stir and she smiles tiredly up at me. "Are you well, my love?"

Nodding, I state quietly, "I'm better than I have ever been before. Your love gives me strength and hope for a happy future."

She immediately begins to sit up. I can tell by the look on her face she is concerned. I press her back down with one hand. "I'm just being introspective this day, my queen. All is well."

She cups my face in her small hands and her gaze turns assessing. "You are okay. I can see it in your face."

"You know me well, my Daisy. Sleep. I will watch over our young one and mull over our future."

She grins and burrows down under my wing again. The warmth of her smaller body pours through me. And my mind travels several parsecs away to our other hatchlings. I'm certain they are well cared for by Roan and his mate. She is probably feeding them piles of doma and laughing while they make a mess of our place. This is our life now. One where warriors look out for each other's young and our queens of our clade genuinely care for one another.

READY FOR MORE SEXY Draconian adventures? Read Draconians Queen (Draconian Warriors Book 6) now!

GLOSSARY

Akes – Draconian god of hunting, war and violence. He is the consort to Entares, the benevolent goddess worshiped by Draconian males.

Antar – Right (Lutar is left.)

Avada – Small carrot-like vegetable that is seasoned and wrapped in a dry leaf.

Challenge –Draconian queens settle disagreements and property disputes by challenging one another in single combat. It is usually a battle to the death.

Clade – Group of Draconians who are descended from a common set of genetic code.

Dark Star – Another term from black hole.

Doma – Type of Draconian flatbread.

Dracon Two – The name the second wave of Draconian warriors nicknamed their new home world. Dracon Two's real name is Onello. It is located in Naxis space. The planet was originally named by Queen Cassandra after a Greek god. It was unofficially renamed Dracon Two because the name their new queen chose is very near the word for feces in the Draconian tongue.

Draconian - Species created by mixing dragon DNA with humanoid DNA. There are many family lines with unique strengths and weaknesses.

Entares – Draconian goddess of beauty, peace and joy. The males worship her as she represents their desire for females to show kindness and respect to them for their many sacrifices, rather than the harsh treatment they normally receive.

Entaza – Dish eaten with the living larva still wiggling in the dish. Common food in Exion space.

Exion – Vast Sector of space encompassing the Draconian home world. Exion is ruled by a race of ruthless females bent on conquest and power.

Hatching – Draconian method of reproduction by which warriors conceive and carry eggs.

Hatchling – Noun: Child. Hatching is a verb: Act of creating young by a male Draconian. Males hatch many times during their lifetimes.

Hatch Mate – Refers to only the children hatched during the same cycle of breeding.

Laser Pistol –A weapon used in battles and self-defense which uses power packs to fire short laser bursts.

Lunar – Equivalent of a complete phase of the primary moon traveling around Dracon One. This is a standard unit of measurement used by many space faring species, even when not on their home planets.

Lutar - Left. (Antar is Right)

Maradox – Queen Ravonda's ship, which was boarded and taken by Queen Cassandra and Mathadar.

Moltan – Malevolent aliens who attack and destroy other vessels.

Naxis – Vast sector of space encompassing five galaxies, including the Milky Way.

Obsidian – The name of a Draconian ship.

Parsec – Unit of distance. Used mostly in determining distance in space.

Parthenogenesis – Draconians males undergo parthenogenesis when exposed to a female's pheromones. It results in them incubating eggs in their bodies which are released into specially designed incubators.

Phase Grenade – Device that sticks to the hull of a ship and disables their weapons.

Revidian – The word used by Draconians to denote a warrior performing oral sex on a queen.

Scion – A word used for offspring, no matter the age.

Solar Revolution – Equivalent of a complete revolution of Dracon One around its sun. This is a standard unit of measurement used by many space faring species, even when not on their home planets.

Sparloc – Aliens aligned with the Moltan in the Naxis sector of space.

Strador Five – Planet populated by amphibians who discovered Earth and decided to abduct human women to sell on the open marketplace.

Strovian – Race of warriors who are at peace with the Draconians in the Naxis sector.

Tarken – Powerfully addicting drug used by queens in the Exion.

Takadon – The Draconian word for a male who is chosen to be the queen's primary breeder. He is to stay at her side constantly and is her protector.

Taladar – Species who initiated a trade agreement with earth to exchange much needed food and other supplies for human brides.

Tankea – Draconian word meaning love between a parent and child or between siblings.

Unders – Anything worn under one's uniform or regular clothing.

Tricon – Unit of thickness.

Utaka Larva – Pupa stage of growth for a tiny colorful flying creatures the Draconians keep for pets.

Vithacan – Symbionts that attach themselves to other creatures and survive off their emotional energy. Soul suckers is a disrespectful term for their race.

Zelerians – Race of squid-like creatures with few humanoid features.

ABOUT THE AUTHOR

Juno Wells grew up on Florida's Space Coast, watching the shuttles take off from Cape Canaveral. When she hit college, her childhood fantasies about space travel turned highly romantic. Now her mind reels with space adventures of fantastic alien lords in distant galaxies, and the earth women they love.

Wells' stories explore the complex, sensual relationships between inhabitants of different star systems. There are always happy endings just as there is always a new world to explore.

Her work is exclusive to Amazon, so read as much as you like with Kindle Unlimited.

www.ingramcontent.com/pod-product-compliance
Lightning Source LLC
Chambersburg PA
CBHW020950180626
46814CB00003B/1025